SINGING WIND

SINGING WIND

RED WITH NATIVE BLOOD

BOOK THREE

MARJORIE CARTER
RANDAL NERHUS

SOUL MISSION PUBLICATIONS

Library of Congress Cataloging-in-Publication. Data is available on file.

ISBN: 9780998717548

Page design by Caryn Pine.

Cover design by Getcovers.

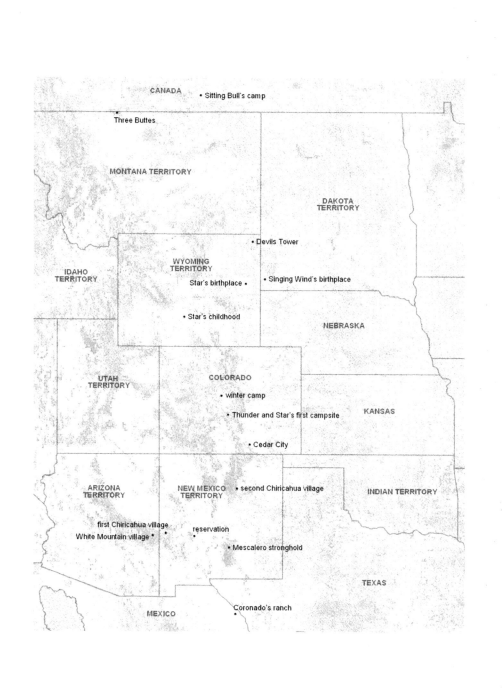

SINGING WIND

Oh, Great spirit
whose voice I hear in the winds,
and whose breath gives life to all the world,
hear me, I am small and weak,
I need your strength and wisdom.

Let me walk in beauty and make my eyes ever
behold the red and purple sunset.
Make my hands respect the things you have made
and my ears sharp to hear your voice.

Make me wise so that I may understand
the things you have taught my people.
Let me learn the lessons you have hidden
in every leaf and rock.

I seek strength, not to be superior to my brother,
but to fight my greatest enemy—myself.
Make me always ready to come to you
with clean hands and straight eyes,
so when life fades, as the fading sunset,
my spirit will come to you without shame.

Lakota Sioux Chief Yellow Lark

ONE

Southwestern Dakota Territory, August 1879

After rising at dawn in her small Sioux village, Singing Wind saw the warriors ride off on another morning hunt.

The sun, a fiery veil of crimson, lit fluffy white clouds drifting lazily across the huge expanse of blue sky. The morning breeze held a pungent mixture of dogwood and paintbrush. Singing Wind thanked the Great Spirit for such a beautiful day.

Kneeling by the stream beside the village, she was washing her mother's doeskin dress when the camp dogs began to yip. Raising her hand to block the sun's glare, Singing Wind saw three braves on foot, naked to the waist, running among the tipis. More men formed a loose circle around the village. Women and children ran crazily about, screaming.

A raid! Run! Cross the stream and hide deep in the briars! Suddenly, strong arms encircled Singing Wind's abdomen, lifting her off the ground. The man's wild war cries nearly deafened her. She dropped the dress, twisted her agile young body, and repeatedly kicked her heels up into her captor's groin. One kick hit its target, and the warrior bellowed and loosened his grip. As she wrenched herself loose, her heart skipped a beat when she recognized the war paint of a Pawnee.

Sprinting away from the man, Singing Wind saw her mother step out of the tipi and look around, bewildered. "Run, Mother!" she screamed frantically. Her mother met her gaze and began to scurry toward her, but a group of Pawnee warriors blocked her mother from view.

Women and children scrambled out of the village, some crossing the creek, others running into the scrub-filled countryside. The sky swarmed with arrows and swinging war clubs. Dodging several Pawnee warriors, she tried desperately to find her mother amid the mayhem. At last, Singing Wind saw her crumpled on the ground, blood dripping from her head, her eyes open and lifeless.

"Mother!" she screamed. Pawnee warriors were everywhere, like wild dogs scattering a herd of defenseless sheep.

A powerful arm encircled Singing Wind's torso, and she blocked the other arm, causing it to slide over her shoulder. When fingers brushed across her mouth, she caught the index finger between her teeth and bit down with all her might. Her captor let out a bloodcurdling howl. Struggling against his bulk, she tried to free herself again. He smashed his fist into the pit of her stomach, sending a cramping pain throughout her abdomen. She fell to the ground, gasping for air.

The captor yipped shrilly, then bound Singing Wind's wrists together. Following the other Pawnee, he dragged her from the village to where the few remaining Sioux horses were tied. He grabbed a bridle lying nearby and deftly slipped it on a horse. After mounting, he pulled her up by her arms, set her in front of him, and rode off.

The sun had grown hot by the time the Pawnee warriors reached an isolated sycamore grove. Singing Wind heard soft nickering through the dense growth. When they came closer, she saw her friends Blue Snow and Blackberry on horseback with their hands tied as well. More Pawnee and horses stood in the cool shade.

Without a word, the warriors dismounted, loosed the pack animals, and led their prisoners into a clearing. They brought forth the bounty from the raid: pots, tools, and valuable jewelry.

As Singing Wind's captor untied the straps around her wrists, she studied him closely. The man's blotchy upper lip only covered part of his long, broken, yellowish teeth, which smelled like something rotten. Saying nothing, he pulled her from the horse and threw her belly-down on a worn-looking mule. The thought of her own death caused her to stay very still while he tied her hands and feet under the mule's ribs. The thin rawhide dug deeply into her wrists and ankles, and she gritted her teeth to keep from crying out. She knew not to make trouble, or the Pawnee would kill her as casually as one might squash a brown beetle.

She recalled many stories about the Pawnee and their brutality. Her great aunt had once seen a warrior bash a baby's head in because it was crying. Just thinking about it caused a chill to pass through her body. Her great aunt had been lucky: her husband, their chief, had paid a large ransom to get her back. Singing Wind knew not to expect such good fortune. With her mother dead, she had no family left.

She watched her captor through the narrow slits of her eyes. The warrior embodied everything she had heard about the cold-blooded Pawnee. In her thirteen winters, she had never before seen such a detestable man. The name "Cruel One" stuck in her mind.

After distributing their loot, the Pawnee mounted up again and rode south. The unrelenting pounding of the mule's hooves against the dry, hard earth bounced Singing Wind's abdomen against its back, wrenching her insides in pain. No mortal could be expected to ride at this pace for so long. Yet across the sweltering plains they rode, alternating between a fast walk and a stomach-jolting trot.

Just after sundown, a brilliant moon rose over the hills, spilling its light across the vast grassland. The rippling grass shimmered like silvery waves of water. Nighthawks swooped across the moon's face like moths over a fire, and wolves called their cries of despair to one another. Singing Wind's flesh crawled at the lonely, wailing sound.

The warriors rode south into the deepening night until the moon stood nearly overhead. Eventually, the leader left the trail and walked his horse through a stand of huge oak trees. The rest followed in single file, threading their way through the timber, dodging low-hanging limbs and waist-high briars.

The wolves' eerie howls grew louder as they moved deeper into the woods. Soon, Singing Wind began to see many shadowy shapes. Tipis stood just beyond a makeshift corral holding hundreds of horses. The howling, she realized, had not been wolves. It had come from the Pawnee scouts that must have been riding ahead of them and stopped at this place.

Cruel One halted, slid from his horse, and walked stiff-legged to join a group of men sprawled around the central campfire. After a short conversation, two men staggered over to Singing Wind and dug their fingers into her wrists and ankles. They unfastened the rough leather straps and flung her legs up, somersaulting her into the air. Her rear slammed against the unforgiving ground, and she bit her lip to keep silent. The braves pulled her arms and legs behind her and retied her aching wrists and ankles once again. She struggled like an upside-down water bug that could not right itself.

The Pawnees' loud laughter echoed in the darkness.

She rocked from side to side until her body flopped to rest on her shoulder and hip. From her new position, she saw many Pawnees seated around a fire.

Halfway through the night, the Pawnee warriors stopped drinking and dragged Blue Snow and Blackberry into the fire-lit circle. Their skin and shredded garments showed marks from beatings. A moment later, when two drunken men came to her, Singing Wind screamed in terror. They grabbed her by her tied arms and legs and swung her into a tree. Her head slammed against the hard trunk, and she lost consciousness.

Floating in and out of dreams, she heard someone killing buffalo. From the cries of pain, she concluded they were doing a poor job of it. Helpless and in too much pain to care, she fell back asleep.

When the tortured cries sounded again, Singing Wind's eyes flew open. She moved her head slightly to seek the source of the noise, and her dream world faded instantly. It was not dying buffalo she had heard, but Blue Snow and Blackberry, stripped naked and bound to stakes in the ground. The girls jerked and twitched as the men on top of them thrust themselves deeper into their torn bodies.

Ignoring the girls' pitiful screams, the other men sat joking and laughing as they waited their turns. Horrified, Singing Wind willed her spirit back into the comforting world of darkness.

She awoke to warm liquid splashing on her face, then recognized the acrid smell of urine. Looking up, she saw a drunken man shake off the last drops before shuffling away. She whipped her head around repeatedly to fling off the stench. Blocking out the pain of her cramping muscles and the disgusting odor, she breathed deeply and slowly. After some time, she fell asleep.

At dawn, the dig of a sharp object into her chest wrenched her back to consciousness. The drunken brave prodded her once more, and she smelled the putrid odor of blood and death tainting the morning air. Still, Singing Wind felt lucky to be alive. She thanked Great Spirit that the Pawnee had not violated her as they had her friends.

Cruel One sauntered over, untied the rawhide binding her ankles, then jerked her bound wrists hard. Upward she came, with sharp pain shooting through every muscle in her body.

Cruel One pulled her past Blue Snow and Blackberry, both dead and lying in blood, their throats slit. Singing Wind cringed in horror. His eyes shot a warning that if she didn't obey, she would meet the same fate. The other warriors, already on their horses, waited. Cruel One tied her belly-down onto the mule again, and they resumed their journey.

Throughout the morning, Singing Wind strained repeatedly to catch a glimpse of Cruel One's back. She kept her spirit alive by thinking how good it would feel to plunge a knife between his sagging shoulders. She yearned to see his blood spurting, to watch him topple face down into the dirt. Hatred kept her strong enough to endure.

At midday, her mule started limping. When Cruel One looked

back and saw the animal lagging behind, he barked an order and the group stopped. With a twisted smile on his face, he pulled out his knife and cut the straps from her wrists and ankles. Singing Wind slid down from the animal and rubbed her wrists. He gave her a cup of water and a handful of dried meat. It was the first food she'd had in two suns. She hid her hatred of him behind a forced smile.

To her dismay, Cruel One removed her mule's halter and drove the animal away with a slap on the buttocks. While walking to Singing Wind, he cut the halter from the lead rope, then knotted it around her neck. After he mounted his gelding, a swift yank on her leash told her she now had to walk. She jolted forward, lights exploding behind her eyes.

Singing Wind recalled her great aunt's stories about the Pawnee. They believed they obtained their sacred power from the god Morning Star. Having provided the first woman to men, that god periodically required them to sacrifice a young virgin in return. Acceding to Morning Star's demand would ensure renewal of life and prevent the earth's destruction by the fire of the sun.

The Pawnee must have chosen me for their next virgin sacrifice. That is why Cruel One gave me food and water: he wanted to be sure I survived the journey. They did not violate me because they want to sacrifice me to the Pawnee god!

Singing Wind tried to recollect what else her great aunt had said about the sacrifice. All she remembered, however, involved the Pawnee placing the girl on a scaffold and shooting her through the heart. She supposed even that would be better than to die the way Blue Snow and Blackberry had. *No! I must find a way to escape!* Against armed warriors on horses, though, it seemed impossible.

On she walked. By early afternoon the heat had grown unbearable and she needed water, but she dared not ask out of terror that Cruel One would notice her stumbling. If she showed weakness, it would provoke him into treating her even more viciously. She forced herself to concentrate on the gently rolling hills and their array of beautiful colors.

As the sun grew even hotter, Singing Wind grew weaker. Facing the dry, ever-blowing wind parched her throat. The intense heat seemed to lull the small group into silence.

A shrill bird's call brought everyone's attention to the warrior who had made it. He pointed to a dark mass on the horizon. *Bluecoats!*

"*Ob-be-mah-e-vah,*" Cruel One snarled at her. He let go of the leash, and she instinctively tumbled behind a bush.

Sounds of whispering floated from nearby bushes. Singing Wind tensed, the thought of escape racing through her mind. She knew it had to be now or never.

It must be now, her spirit told her. *Now, while they cannot shoot without alerting the soldiers.* If Cruel One found her, he would kill her in a mad rage. Nevertheless, she would prefer a quick death over being sacrificed to the hungry Pawnee god.

She coiled the leash in her hand and began to crawl across the hot sand. *Any moment, Cruel One will grab my hair and wrench my head back.* She could almost feel the blade of his knife sliding across her throat.

Singing Wind kept crawling at a daring pace, stopping only briefly to look over her shoulder. To her relief, she saw no one. A dash of hope stirred in the depths of her soul. *Move away from the soldiers and the Pawnee dogs,* her spirit whispered. She continued slithering across the sandy terrain like a gigantic snake, making no sound save the soft rumbling in her breast as she chanted her prayers:

> Spirit of an eagle, see me, help me,
> Send brother wolf with eyes to see,
> Send brother bear to set me free.
>
> Spirit of an eagle, see me, help me,
> Send brother tree that I might hide,
> Send brother horse for me to ride.
>
> Spirit of an eagle, see me, help me,
> Send sister rain to fill my tracks,
> Send brother arrow to Pawnee backs.
>
> Spirit of an eagle, hear me,
>
> Spirit of an eagle, help me,
>
> Spirit of an eagle, save me.

Singing Wind's prayers were answered. When the first gunshots erupted, she sprang to her feet and ran for her life.

TWO

New Mexico Territory, August 1879

The land had grown steep and rocky over the last few miles, slowing Sanchez, José, and Paco to a turtle's pace. Sanchez would have stopped if the sun had not already risen because he worried about breaking the fine-boned legs of his two mares. He did not care so much about the mule he rode. It was accustomed to carrying his overweight body.

As the sun grew higher, the land became gentler and finally leveled off. Neat hedgerows began marking off cultivated fields, and a sparkling stream circled lazily through green pastures. In the distance, Sanchez spotted a herd of longhorn cattle grazing contentedly. Then, he caught sight of the fort, swelling from a dot on the horizon into a solid wall of timber.

At the huge wooden gates of the fort, a freckle-faced boy of seven or eight years ran out to them. "Morning, sir. Y'all look plumb tuckered out and so do your horses. If you need water, there's a cistern right over there and a trough for your horses too."

"*Gracias, nene.* Can you tell me where the man in charge lives?" Relieved he had reached the fort and encountered someone helpful, Sanchez looked forward to washing up and finding rest. But there was still business to do, and his own comfort would wait until after he spoke to the officer.

"Sure, Mister. My father's Captain Baker, and he's at home right now." The boy pointed to a well-kept cabin several yards away. "I'll tell him he has visitors." Sanchez watched as the boy ran to the house.

A moment later, the captain walked out, smiling. He greeted the travelers and invited them to have a seat on the front porch. He told the boy to ask his mother to bring the coffee pot and three more cups. The boy went inside, and a moment later, a woman came through the door bearing a laden tray.

"How can I help you gentlemen?" the captain asked as he filled the cups and passed them around the table.

"*Señor* Captain," Sanchez said, "we were returning home from a trading trip when two Indian girls came into our camp." A frown deepened Sanchez's chubby cheeks as he told Baker how the girls had tricked him, then stolen his servants. "They also burned all my trade goods. We were still in the territory riddled with Mescaleros when we met Sergeant Clark. He told us he and his men were looking for the same girls. He promised to bring the girls here, and I hope he'll bring my servants too."

Captain Baker struggled to understand Sanchez's story. "You say the thieves were two Indian girls?"

"*Sí,* but these girls are not average squaws. They're the devil's spawn!"

"When Clark returns with your property and servants, we'll return them to you," the captain said, suppressing the urge to smile. Sanchez's story sounded familiar, very much like Sergeant O'Riley's. He felt sincerely sorry for the merchant's loss, but the situation was not without a touch of humor. He actually found himself hoping Clark would bring the girls in alive. He looked forward to meeting them.

The captain rose early the next morning. As he took his first sip of coffee, he thought of Sergeant Clark. He had taken his men far too close to the dreaded Mescaleros. The captain finished his breakfast and hurried to his office, where he sent his aide to find Barney and Lieutenant Jackson.

Barney stepped into the captain's office minutes later, and the two waited for Jackson. When the lieutenant finally arrived, the captain noticed sleep in his eyes and his wrinkled clothing. *Probably yesterday's uniform.*

"Lieutenant," the captain said, "I'm concerned about Sergeant Clark and his squad. I sent him out to capture the two Indian girls who have caused so much trouble around here. From what I learned from a Mexican trader yesterday, Clark is dangerously close to the Mescalero stronghold. If you follow the Mexican's tracks south, you should find his squad easily. Take over his command and add his men to yours."

"Yes, sir. When would you like me to go?"

"Now. And you'd better watch yourself, Lieutenant. I hear the girls are pretty damned tricky."

Barney spoke up. "Them 'paches is growed up fer war just like them gol-dang Comanches, sir. They been a-fighting somebody off this here land fer hundreds a' years. Best ya be looking south of the border. Them danged redskins done stole so many women they be kin to half the Mexicans between here and Sonora."

The captain laughed. "Thank you, Barney, for that useful information."

"You orta not be laughing at me, sir, or at them Injuns neither. Them 'paches is thick out there, just like skeeters and snakes. All us ol' trappers knows they's the biggest hazard of doin' business in the badlands. An' 'em youngsters you sent out the other day with the sergeant got a lot a learnin' afore they can find an Apache, much less ketch one, sir."

"All right, Lieutenant," said the captain. "Why don't you just take Barney and his superior knowledge on the patrol with you? And issue him a horse. He'd have a hard time keeping up with the rest of you on his burro."

"Yes, sir," the lieutenant said with a smart salute. He hurried down the steps, embarrassed the captain had seen him hungover and still in the clothes he had slept in. He had never drunk so much back East. This godforsaken place was enough to drive any man to drink.

THREE

New Mexico Territory, August 1879

The air thickened and became humid. Hope filled the hearts of Thunder and her followers as they tramped through the night. But with the rising sun, the promise of rain died. Still, the sight of a road elated the footsore travelers. Hardly a real road, it consisted of two narrow strips where wagon wheels had killed the prairie grass.

The haggard group dropped onto the hot, dry earth to rest. After a brief exchange of opinions, everyone agreed it would be wiser to follow the trail. However, they would have to stay on guard for passing wagon trains.

The northeastward path led them into a country of low, rust-colored hills. Yucca dotted the land, and birds began to appear. In the distance, the ground rose higher. Hope soared in their hearts again. The desert would soon give way to the hills and green valleys of the mountains.

Late morning, as Thunder led the band up a slope, she felt the ground softer under her feet. Many steps later, mud caking to her moccasins brought forth a surge of exhilaration.

"It rained here last night!"

After some time, Stormy threw his head back and whinnied. He galloped into low-lying woodland, followed by the thirsty travelers. Flashes of a glistening river shone between the trees! The group rushed ahead giving it their all—but none could muster more than a half trot. They clumsily made their way to its bank and dropped to their knees. Plunging their heads into the river, they sucked in the fresh, revitalizing water.

Thunder's parched tongue and palate tingled as the water came rushing in. She swallowed rapaciously, the first gulp of cool liquid inching its way down and spilling into her stomach. *Thank you, Great One, for the life-giving water!* Taking swallow after swallow, she finally forced herself to stop. Lifting her head, she took a deep breath and whispered, "Thank you, Grandfather, for guiding us here."

Star sat nearby, flinging her long, wet hair away from her face as the others continued guzzling. "Everybody stop drinking!" Star shouted. Thunder quickly translated her words into Spanish.

Victoria and the Mescaleros slowly raised their faces from the stream. The men stood and walked to the horses. They patted the horses' flanks as they took the ropes from the saddles, slung them around the animals' necks, and pulled them back from the stream. Maria, however, still drank deeply.

Thunder knew Star was right. "Maria, you must stop now!" She ran to her, grabbed her shoulders, and pulled her back from the stream.

Maria yanked Thunder's hair with her left hand and swung to slap her with her right. "Just let me drink!"

Thunder blocked the blow. "You have had enough, Maria!"

"I have not!" Maria yelled, kicking at Thunder. "Leave me alone!"

Thunder peeled Maria's grip from her hair and pushed her to the ground. "If you drink any more, you will get sick and die!"

Maria said nothing. She stared coldly at Thunder, on the verge of fighting her way back to the stream to quench her voracious thirst.

"Maria," Star said, "please fetch the bag of salt *Señor* Coronado gave us." As she spoke, Thunder calmed herself and translated Star's instructions. "Pour half the salt in a cooking bowl and give it to the Mescaleros for the horses. Then, give each of us a handful. We must take in salt as we drink."

Maria slowly stood and walked to the mule. Victoria followed, knowing she would need to calm her daughter. Grateful for Thunder's and Star's concern, she smiled, thinking their knowledge always surprised her.

As Maria pulled the provisions from the pack, Victoria put her hand on her shoulder. "I know you were spellbound at the stream, Maria—I could barely take my mouth from the water too. Only *Señorita* Thunder's concern for your life caused her to pull you away from the river."

"I never thought water could kill me," Maria said as she took out the bag of salt. "My thirst has lessened now. I'll try to let it pass."

By mid-afternoon, they all gradually drank until everyone had their fill. Exhaustion now replacing their thirst, they scattered and prepared to nap in the shade along the river.

Thunder and Star walked a few steps upriver to a pine tree. As they settled at its base, Star said, "We have returned Roberto and found our way out of the desert. I am ready to help you find Golden Eagle if you wish."

The offer left Thunder flustered. "No," she whispered. "I am not ready to find him yet."

Carefully, Star asked, "What do you fear about finding him?"

Star's question pierced the center of Thunder's pain, and rage surged through her.

"The trapper violated me," she fumed, "and I hate living this way. I see myself finding Golden Eagle and feeling only shame when he learns of my defilement."

Star nodded. "Your people live by traditions from times before the whites came here. Tradition cannot guide us in everything. The whites are taking and destroying all we have, and this forces us to see beyond our traditions."

Would Golden Eagle think the same way? Thunder asked herself. Her warrior spirit gave the answer: *Whether he would or not, I will not let this shame consume my life. Yet, how can I prevent it?* To her surprise, she recalled how she had felt no shame for days in the desert. *All my worries vanished when my mind was set on survival. How real are they?* With that thought, she lay down and rested.

The late afternoon sun had moved beyond the pine branches, its rays shining on Thunder's face when she awoke. She looked over at Star, to find her still asleep in the shade. Something unknown kept tugging at the back of her mind, making her restless. She rose, left the campsite, and slipped upstream.

The river here was much wider, the current slower. Huge cottonwoods grew from the banks, their limbs drooping into the dark, shadowy waters. An air of menace hung about the place, as if it harbored secrets.

Thunder stripped off her dress, washed it, and hung it on a nearby bush. She stepped into the cool water, walking carefully across the river bottom to avoid cutting her feet on the sharp rocks. Her movement caused mud to rise in giant mushroom clouds around her legs. In the middle of the river she paused, enjoying the water as it lapped against her bare body.

Images of Golden Eagle ran through her mind. She had not thought of him as they journeyed in the desert's torturous heat. But here, in the cool of the river, Thunder remembered him and felt momentarily content. After growing accustomed to the chill of the water, she closed her eyes. The gentle rippling motion rocked her until a vision of Golden Eagle appeared. She felt his arms reaching around her, bringing serenity to her inner being, and she shivered with exquisite delight.

"He is near," she whispered, then opened her eyes and searched the surrounding red hills. Several times she thought she saw him, but it was always a phantom, a trick of the light, or of her own mind. No, she decided, she saw nothing to confirm her feelings.

I may never see Golden Eagle again.

Depressed, she diverted her attention to trying to catch a sluggish, bloated fish. With her hands and mind moving in different directions, though, the fish simply swam away.

Thunder studied the hills once more. They bulged like sleeping monsters in the sunshine. She shifted her gaze to the stream, alarmed to see the head of a venomous water moccasin gliding along the rippled surface. Only paces away, the snake darted toward her, too quickly for her to flee. She stood petrified, not allowing a muscle to twitch. Closing her eyes, she wished for Star's rapport with animals.

When she could no longer stand the suspense, she opened her eyes. The olive-brown serpent floated within arm's reach. Suddenly, its head submerged, its body following downward until it disappeared. Thunder felt the snake's icy coldness slither against her leg. Fear filled her with self-loathing, and she thought herself unworthy as a warrior. Motionless, she awaited the sting of the snake's bite. When she caught a brief glimpse of it slithering away, she sighed in blessed relief.

Shadows overtook the water rippling against the bank, and Thunder realized she had lost all track of time. The day had almost passed. Dusk covered the land, as if someone had blown out the fire in the sun. She waded back to the bank, and dressed.

When she returned, everyone was sitting together talking. Star looked at her intently and asked, "Did you enjoy your swim?"

She knows what happened, Thunder realized. "A water moccasin nearly bit me."

"At that moment, you wished for my power to ward off the snake." Thunder heard a reassuring note in Star's tone.

Star smiled as she slowly rose. "Thunder, let us find some herbs that will help our bodies adjust to eating and drinking again." They walked away together.

"What do you suppose she meant about power?" Yellow Dog asked Victoria.

"I don't know. I don't speak that language."

Yellow Dog translated the conversation for Victoria and Maria, then said, "Many seasons ago, a trader came to our village. He told a story about a young Cheyenne Holy Girl who had been born under a falling star. Their shaman predicted the girl would become a great healer and leader." He paused, lowering his voice. "Do you think...?"

"Thunder introduced her as Falling Star," Maria reminded him reverently.

Bear Claw, a fearful expression on his face, whispered, "We should try to escape!" Supernatural power terrified nearly all Apaches, and the people endowed with it scared them even more.

Yellow Dog shook his head in disagreement. "Escape? Why? We are not prisoners, and in these first suns of freedom, no safer place exists than with a Holy One. It doesn't matter if she is Cheyenne, or a girl, so long as she communes with the spirits. I am staying. Bear Claw, you and Turtle can do as you wish."

Yellow Dog saw his friends grow calmer. Apparently, they took his words to heart.

Star and Thunder returned and persuaded the others to move the camp upstream to where she had bathed. Everyone worked together and soon packed all their belongings on the horses.

On the way there, Star pointed. "Look ahead. Our trail meets with a more heavily traveled road that crosses the stream."

"We will need to watch out for anyone passing through," Thunder responded, "while we eat, rest, and hunt."

"Good, I am very hungry. Can Victoria fix cactus tonight?"

After Thunder translated, Victoria picked up the machete and headed to a nearby prickly pear patch. Maria joined her. They didn't know exactly what a Holy Girl was, but they definitely wanted to remain on Star's good side.

The next morning, Bear Claw and Thunder came back from a hunt, with an antelope carcass on Stormy's back. Everyone helped Victoria slice the meat and hang the surplus on bushes to dry. After cooking and eating the rest, they sat by the fire, licking fat from their fingers and discussing what dangers might lie ahead.

Thunder announced that Star, Maria, and Victoria needed to learn how to use guns, and the trio reluctantly agreed. Thunder and the Mescaleros collected all the weapons and Coronado's ammunition. As they searched their stock, Thunder was happy to find that all the rifles, including the trapper's rifle, were Winchesters, which used the same shells. The Mescaleros dug through the variety of bullets in the saddlebags until they found a few handfuls for the Colt .45.

The Mescaleros rode out in three directions to keep watch. Thunder loaded the guns, then gave Star and Maria each a rifle, and Victoria the pistol.

As they practiced, Thunder remembered what the soldiers had done to her people. She told the others of her village's fate and of her vow of revenge. While talking about how good it would feel to kill Polecat, she saw a look of horror on Victoria's face. Surprised by Victoria's reaction, Thunder fell silent. *Best to pursue my vengeance by only telling Star. Yet even she does not agree.* With that thought, Thunder ended the lesson.

The next morning at dawn, everyone awoke to the sound of cattle bawling. Thunder had a queasy stomach. *Probably from eating too much antelope yesterday. No time to deal with it now.*

Through the trees, they saw a herd of longhorns, followed by cowhands, moving across the distant hills. Moments later, a group of fourteen soldiers rendezvoused with the cowpokes, who then drove the cattle to a ford in the river.

"Thunder," Star said, "we have plenty of time to avoid the soldiers by leaving now. We can hide in the mountains upstream."

"No. It would be to our best advantage to fight here," Thunder said. *We should be back in the same fort's territory as my last village. Chances are good Polecat is among them.*

The soldiers rode into a valley between hills, vanishing from sight until they reappeared, riding two abreast. The lead pair halted on the ridge and stared down at the river.

"If the soldiers come close enough to discover us," Thunder told everyone, "they will die. Men, tie the horses securely and be sure the weapons are ready for battle. Star, follow me. Yesterday, I saw a hill where we can waylay them."

They walked to the road, turned onto it, and crossed the shallow river. After ascending a small hill, they looked down to a narrow point in the road. Only wide enough for two horsemen to ride side by side, the pathway formed a shallow groove through the land. On both sides rose chest-high banks and wild growth tall enough to conceal attackers. Thunder almost dreaded entering the death trap, an ideal spot for an ambush.

Upon reaching the far end of the passageway, they found themselves at the foot of a long pine-covered hill. Thunder's hair whipped across her face from a strong north wind. *As we shoot, even the smoke from our guns will be carried out of our way. Excellent!*

"It looks like a tunnel into the underworld," Thunder whispered nervously. "I can almost feel the demons watching me. But it is a good spot and should serve our purpose well. Slip back, get the guns, and tell the others I've found the perfect trap."

"We still have time enough to safely ride away," Star said. "Victoria, Maria, and I have not had much practice shooting, and we would be of little or no use."

"Why run away when we can kill the soldiers right here? We have four good shots. You three do not have to fight if you do not want to."

"Four against fourteen?"

Thunder thought for a moment. "Each of us could kill four without difficulty."

"You still have not recovered from the trapper's attack. It is not wise to fight here. Think about it."

"I am not running into the mountains like a coward."

"Thunder, you are crazy!" Star rolled her eyes and left for camp.

Thunder pushed back her stomach's urge to vomit, walked into the brush, and found the best position to observe the road from ample cover. *Crazy or not, I will not pass up my chance.*

Star got the others and returned. Thunder divided them into two groups. She took Victoria, Maria, and Bear Claw with her to the east side of the road. Star, Turtle, and Yellow Dog hid to the west.

Yellow Dog, acting as scout, concealed himself in the place Thunder had chosen. He had felt useless doing woman's work in the field, so he now bore his responsibility proudly. He would give the signal to begin the assault. The position of trust made him feel like a true Mescalero.

The perfection of the trap made the fate of the soldiers seem to Thunder like a foregone conclusion. She and the others had barely taken their stations when Yellow Dog signaled, *They enter.*

During the ensuing wait, the very trees seemed to cease their rustling. The silence grew oppressive, as in the eye of a storm. Hiding behind a boulder among the bushes, Thunder saw the first two soldiers round the curve and fought the urge to hold her breath.

The first pair, each armed with a rifle and pistol, rode stirrup to stirrup. They advanced trotting, then slowed as they rode up the stony incline. The other soldiers—riding with ease and cockiness —followed two by two in close formation.

With great effort, Thunder forced her eyes away from the soldiers. She glanced across the roadway to the hiding places of the Mescaleros.

By the time the last two riders entered the trap, the first pair was approaching the crucial center of the ambuscade. Thunder tried to gauge the soldiers as one unit, but her eyes kept returning unbidden to the lead pair. The last few moments of waiting were sheer agony. For the Bluecoats to see them too soon would mean certain death.

"Strike true the first time," Thunder mouthed to Maria and Victoria. "You may not have a second chance."

Thunder studied the soldiers in the trap. *The lead pair are directly in front of me only a few paces away, but others are too far back to tell if Polecat is among them. If so, he will die!* Not caring of her peril, Thunder stepped out of the thicket, screamed the Apache war cry, and took aim at the leader.

Another rider, only a few paces away, drew his pistol and fired point-blank. Pain ripped through the fleshy part of Thunder's upper arm, and she dropped her rifle. Off balance and hearing bullets zipping past, she picked up the gun and saw the Mescaleros shoot three soldiers from their horses. Maria fired at the man nearest them, missing every shot. It took all of Thunder's fortitude to raise her wounded arm, but no amount of pain would stop her from killing Bluecoats. She rested her rifle on the boulder and shot two. The closest soldier again pulled the pistol's trigger, but the gun failed to fire. Before Thunder could take aim, the young man hurled his pistol at her. The gun slammed against her forehead.

Pain and a burst of bright colors consumed her mind, and she felt very lightheaded.

The panicked soldier shrieked, "It's those savage sisters!" He slid from his horse and sprinted off as she lost consciousness.

Lying out of sight of the others, Thunder returned to awareness feeling pain in her shoulder and hip. Blood ran from her shoulder, and she ground her teeth together to keep from crying out.

"Every soldier dead!" Yellow Dog declared. The firing had ceased, and the odor of smoke had begun to clear. Everyone else stood silent, looking upon the gruesome death scene before them.

Star looked around puzzled. "Where is Thunder?"

Before Thunder could respond, Maria cried, "Thunder, where are you?"

"Over here!" Thunder yelled. "I have been shot." Clutching her bleeding shoulder, she sat up and noticed a small bloodstained area at her waist. Her skin had been cut, and so had her dress and arrowhead pouch. *Too small for a bullet wound.* Looking back, she saw a sharp rock protruding from the ground and realized the pouch had protected her. It still bulged from the arrowheads inside; she could repair it later.

Maria arrived, stared at Thunder, and whispered in a worried voice, "Blessed Mary, Holy Mother of Jesus." Then, she shouted, "Star, come quick!"

Star sprinted to Thunder's side, her face flushed with apprehension.

"My wound is not serious," Thunder told her. "What about the rest of you?"

"We are all fine," Star assured her. Maria and Star helped her struggle to her feet and shuffle to the roadway, where downed troopers lay scattered. She wondered if Polecat lay among the dead.

Maria left Thunder's side, ran to the dead soldiers, and started kicking them. "*¡Las ratas!*" she shrieked. "*¡Tus ratas dañaron a mi amiga!*"

"What is she saying?" Star asked Thunder as they followed Maria.

"She called the dead men rats for hurting me," Seeing Maria kicking the bodies made Thunder laugh in gratification. She hovered over the soldiers, savoring the sweet taste of revenge. "I have taken these lives to free the souls of my people." She surveyed the dead, but to her disappointment, she did not see Polecat.

Yellow Dog asked, "Should we go after the soldier who escaped?"

Thunder thought for a moment. "No. Let him go back and tell the others that they will die if they invade Apache land."

Yellow Dog flashed her a toothy grin. "You are a true warrior; a warrior like the ancients who first fought their way up through a hole in the earth."

"Should we bury the bodies?" Turtle asked.

"No," she said with disgust. "Let them rot in the sun. Collect their bullets and whatever else we can use from their gear."

Yellow Dog nodded, and the Mescaleros busied themselves removing scalps and severing each soldier's ligaments, so they could not fight in the next life.

"What are they doing?" Maria asked.

"The Apache have a complex tradition of counting coup," Thunder explained. "They reward a warrior who strikes a live enemy for his exceptional bravery. The Apache also regard scalping as a coup, a ritual to win prestige. The scalps symbolize the souls of one's enemies, who will become slaves of the victors in the next life."

Maria nodded and grinned, apparently impressed.

Star sat Thunder down, cleaned her wound, and wrapped it in cloth. "You can be grateful the bullet went through muscle and did not shatter a bone. What about the bump on your forehead, and the cut on your waist?"

"There is no time to fix them now, savage sister. We must go before others come."

"'Savage sister'?"

"Early in the battle, a soldier called us 'the savage sisters.'"

The others looked on questioningly.

Thunder grinned and repeated the phrase in Spanish for the benefit of Victoria and Maria.

"The savage sisters?" Maria asked, bug-eyed. "Is that who you are?"

Everyone laughed.

As Star went to call the horses to her, Victoria and Maria started back to camp to pack the belongings.

"I killed this one!" Maria bragged.

"Hush, Maria!" Victoria scolded. "You are becoming more like *Señorita* Thunder every day."

"The Mescaleros killed all the others," Maria continued with admiration, "except the two Thunder got. When the Mescaleros used up their bullets, they broke cover and killed the last three soldiers with their bare hands!"

Visibly irate and disappointed with her daughter's enthusiasm for killing, Victoria went back to camp and prepared for travel.

The group mounted and fled north along the river with their newfound bounty of horses. While riding, Yellow Dog recounted the details of the battle to Thunder. He told her, other than Maria's one lucky shot, the new shooters had hit nothing.

It will take many more suns to train them, Thunder reflected, *so we must resume lessons soon.*

They rode on until midday, when Star forced everyone to stop so she could tend to Thunder's wounds properly. While the others prepared a meal, Star drew Thunder aside and extended her hand. "Swallow these mountain laurel seeds—they will help deaden your pain."

Thunder took them and frowned. "They are poisonous."

"If you eat too many. This is just enough to keep you from hurting."

Reluctantly, Thunder threw the seeds in her mouth, opened her canteen, and washed them down. They went to the riverbank where Thunder sat on a large rock in the shade. Star delicately removed the cloth bandage from her shoulder. Next, she took crushed lantana leaves from her herb pouch and animal fat from a clay jar, then mixed them together.

"You almost got us all killed," Star said nonchalantly.

Thunder looked at Star with eyes wide open. "Did I?"

"We were supposed to wait for Yellow Dog's signal."

Thunder sat with mouth agape, remembering only that she was ready to die.

"Then you needlessly exposed yourself before aiming at the soldiers."

I should have stayed hidden and had my rifle aimed before giving my war cry. Star is right. Why was I so careless? Then, she confessed, "When I was under the trapper, I prayed to the spirits to let me survive. I agreed to accept death soon afterward, in battle or from illness."

"You were not just accepting death today," Star said as she daubed the salve on Thunder's shoulder. "You were inviting it. Does your whole heart wish for you to die?" She wrapped the shoulder in a strip of cloth.

"Part of me wishes that."

"Only a part of you," Star emphasized. She scooped up a handful of clay from the river's edge. "At the center of our hearts, we never wish to punish or destroy ourselves. There, we know we do not deserve it."

Thunder nodded. "I was so eager to kill Polecat that I was not thinking clearly..." Her words trailed off as she thoughtlessly looked toward the horizon.

Star worked the moist clay into a flat disk. "As a warrior, you must think clearly. The spirits will not hold you to the bargain you made. They wish you to thrive every day you live." She pressed the clay disk over Thunder's bound shoulder.

"If that is true, they will help me in my vengeance."

Star sighed. "It seems odd to me that your thoughts are so different from your actions."

"What do you mean?"

"You took pity on the first white person you encountered after the trapper's attack." Star covered the clay with another layer of cloth. "You spared the sentry's life, did you not?"

"He seemed innocent, so just silencing him felt right."

Star rose, walked around Thunder, and looked into her eyes. "Then you returned a young boy to his home and freed slaves. Are those the actions of one filled with a need for vengeance? Does it not satisfy you deeply to fight for the helpless, and does needless bloodshed not torment you?"

Thunder shrugged with her good shoulder. "I have not thought much about that, Star. Other thoughts have filled my mind."

"Why not start now?" Star stepped closer and pressed the palm of her hand on the bandage.

"For what happened to me and my people, they all deserve to die!"

Star increased pressure on the bandage. "Then why did you spare the sentry when you had planned to kill him?"

Thunder's mind calmed as she felt warmth seeping through the bandage. "He did not seem anything like Polecat or the trapper."

"Think about the dead soldiers. Can you see them, too, the same as the sentry?" Star drew back her hand and walked to camp.

Thunder's shoulder felt much better. She recalled her frenzied state after the battle. And now she envisioned the dead soldiers more clearly. None were like Polecat or the trapper. Remembering she could have avoided the battle, a pang of guilt struck her. Vengeance lost its grip until she thought of Polecat. She gritted her teeth. *Killing him alone would satisfy me.*

As they rode, the land grew more level and the air cooled, allowing them to travel rapidly.

At dawn of the second day, Victoria and Maria had the morning meal ready. Again, Thunder had an uneasy stomach. As the band sat around the campfire eating, Thunder took little food and ate sparingly, trying not to bring attention to herself. Once everything was packed, and all had mounted, Thunder told Yellow Dog, "Lead us since you know the territory, and I will bring up the rear."

While the others rode safely ahead, Thunder twisted over the side of Stormy and vomited. For so many days she had undergone jolting horseback riding, hunger, thirst, and deadly battles. Yet nothing she did could rid her body of the baby she carried. She had missed her time of bleeding half a moon after the trapper's attack, and now missed another one. She wanted to tell Star but could not bring herself to do it. *Star will just tell me to keep the baby. I will begin to show soon. Maybe then I will be ready to talk to her about it.* She continued riding in silence. *No, I will not be ready*, she finally admitted to herself. *But I will not have a choice.*

Two suns later, they reached the foot of the Sacramento Mountains.

In late afternoon, they saw a westward-leading path that the Mescaleros recognized immediately. Upon hearing their excited whooping, Thunder whispered a prayer of thanks to her grandfather's spirit.

The group halted at the road's divide. Thunder looked at Yellow Dog. "Parting with such good friends pains me. Let us share our bounty. So many animals may lead to our capture. We could never cover the trail of this herd. We will keep three for packhorses. Take what horses and guns you need, and half the ammunition."

Yellow Dog smiled. "Our village has enough land for the horses we are riding, along with three more and the mule."

"Good," Star said. "If the soldiers find some horses, they may assume we have freed all of them."

After dismounting, the three Mescaleros took the rifles and bullets, then tied lead ropes to the animals and remounted.

"If you wish," Yellow Dog offered, "we will help you find Star's people."

"*Muchas gracias, amigos,*" Thunder said. "We appreciate your offer, but what lies ahead is our duty, not yours. Do not worry. We will ride in haste, and you should do the same. When the cavalry finds the dead soldiers, they will send many more after the killers."

"Yes, I agree," Turtle said as he and the other Mescaleros led the mule and Army horses. "The three of us will leave separately and meet at the road many bowshots west. If you use the remaining horses to blot out our tracks before you free them, it will slow the Bluecoats."

"Consider it done," Thunder answered. "May Father Sun rest lightly on your backs."

"And may the spirits ride with you on your journey," Yellow Dog said. "We shall never forget that we owe you our freedom. If you ever need us, we will be here."

The Mescaleros rode off, continuing to wave intermittently until they faded into the shadows of the Sacramento Mountains.

FOUR

Nebraska, August 1879

The morning after her escape, Singing Wind awoke to the sun casting its first light on the grass-covered countryside. As she looked around, the leash rubbed against her chafed neck. She sat up and started loosening the knot. To her relief, she saw no signs of Pawnee warriors or soldiers. *I am safe for now, but maybe the Pawnee are tracking me.*

Very thirsty and hungry, she planned to backtrack along the route the Pawnee had taken. She remembered on the day of her capture, her people's hunters had not seen buffalo for many suns. The band planned to move their camp two suns travel to the north to find more buffalo. Once she returned to familiar land, she could easily find her tribe's new campsite.

At last, she worked the knot open and pulled off the leash. *We crossed a creek yesterday, not long before sundown.* She got up, flung the leash behind her, and started walking.

Thoughts of the morning when the Pawnee warriors had attacked her village brought back memories of Blue Snow and Blackberry. Images of them writhing under those filthy men tore at Singing Wind's soul. She shivered violently and swallowed, trying to rid herself of the feeling of hands wrapped around her own throat.

At mid-morning, she was elated to find the creek. She drank until she slaked her thirst then hurriedly bathed. While donning her clothes she spotted a deer antler in the brush. Her people always considered antlers a sign of luck. It would have many uses, so she took it with her. Finding chokecherries growing along the stream she ate as many of the ripe black ones as she could and spit out the poisonous seeds. After harvesting the ripest cherries she could easily carry, she moved on.

For three suns, Singing Wind endured hunger, heat, and cold as she trudged northward. She made every effort to hide her trail by walking through water or thickets. On the afternoon of the fourth day, the sight of the Black Hills restored her bearings, and she came upon a river flowing east. She ran along its bank, sure that her people's camp lay farther downstream. Finally, at dusk under an overcast sky, she lay down and slept.

Waking at dawn, she noticed a storm building to the northwest, and resumed her search. At midmorning, she saw the expected encampment, but no tipis stood in the area. Puzzled, she carefully walked through the grounds seeing partially burnt logs at the spent fires, as if the people had left in a hurry. A small roll of string lay near a fire, and she put it in her pocket, knowing it would be useful. Looking over the campsite under dark clouds, she spied a half-buried piece of deerskin and picked it up. *A baby's moccasin.* She recognized the beaded decoration. *It is Little Deer's. She always kicks them off.* Inspecting the ground more closely, she found indentations similar to hoof marks, but wider and deeper than any normal horse could make. The tracks headed northeast, in the direction from which they had come. She saw a curved piece of metal and picked it up. Studying it, she remembered the warriors' stories about metal shoes that soldiers put on their horses' hooves. *Soldiers have taken my people to a reservation!*

Hope swelled within as she thought of following the tracks and easily finding her people. But suddenly a cold gust of wind blew across the vacant campsite, and fat raindrops began to pelt her. Singing Wind ran to the river and took cover under an evergreen tree. It provided little shelter since the wind blew the heavy rain in all directions.

The rain pounded the land for a long time. Singing Wind knew the downpour would erase the tracks leading to her people. Envisioning the huge reservation to the northeast, she doubted she could find her people without tracks to lead her to them. She recalled hearing that the soldiers at the reservations took no pity on lone, homeless tribespeople. She could not risk ending up in a situation worse than her current straits. With winter only a few moons away, she needed to find a place to survive. She remembered stories of mountains far to the west. Game still thrived there, but winters gripped that land as harshly as her own. Other tales told of the territory to the south, where it seldom froze or snowed. She did not know whether those dry mountains produced game, but she hoped she could survive the milder winter there. Maybe some village in that land would allow her to live with them. Often praised by her people for her hard work, she felt confident she could prove her worthiness. When spring returned, she would decide what to do next.

How could she survive long enough to reach that land? Her people relied on buffalo for sustenance, but she could not possibly kill even one by herself. After her father's death two years ago, she had ridden his horse to where game abounded, hunting with her bow for antelope and prairie dogs to provide for her mother and herself. That became much more difficult two moons back, when her horse died of colic. From then on, she caught fish for food. If she could make a knife, she would use it to make snares and fish traps.

When the storm passed, Singing Wind shed her clothes, wrung them out, and left them in the sun to dry. She decided to use the horseshoe and the antler to make a knife blade of flint. She went to the stream, found a good stone for the purpose, and sat. Resting the stone on her leg, she struck it with the horseshoe until breaking off a long sliver of the proper width, then scraped the edge into a knife arc. It took some effort with the antler before she found proper angle to chip the stone into a sharp edge.

Using her newly crafted blade, she sawed a branch from a sapling, cut it to the length of a handle, and carved a notch into its end. The flint blade fit snugly into the notched branch, making a knife. After cutting some string from the roll, she bound the knife handle to the flint blade. The brittleness of the blade would require her to use it with great care.

As she had hardly eaten for days, she cut branches to use for a fish trap. Wading into the river, she found a sandbank that funneled water into a narrow passage. Planting the sticks into the mud, she formed a pattern like a flock of migrating geese. She then positioned the rest of the sticks in two curved arcs, leaving only a small opening between them. She returned to camp, donned her clothes, and slept.

The next morning, she returned to her trap, and to her delight, she found a large catfish. She caught it by its gills, dismantled the stick trap, and returned to camp. The roasted fish was the tastiest she had ever eaten. After filling her stomach, she began her journey south, across the grassland.

Long days passed as Singing Wind walked in solitude. Every night at sundown, she stopped to set fish traps and snares, then cooked and ate her catches in the mornings. If she caught nothing, she ate nuts, berries, and whatever else she could forage.

She drove onward by telling herself that she walked, not on hard ground, but rather in a special place above. *A sacred place without pain, between Father Sky and Mother Earth.*

"I am Lakota Sioux, a blood Sioux," she told the rocks and lizards. "My name is Singing Wind, and like the wind, my feet do not touch the ground." Hearing her own words, she spontaneously straightened her back and strengthened her stride. She had, after all, outsmarted the Pawnee!

One night when Singing Wind could bear no more, she dragged her exhausted body into a deep ravine. One moon had passed since her escape from the Pawnee. Finding no water to bathe with, she brushed the dirt from her bare legs and straightened her long braids. After wiping the sweat from her face, she curled up on a large, flat rock to sleep. Thousands of years of water and sand had polished the stone as smooth as marble. She did not notice its beauty, nor did she see the blood-red sunset. She could only think of rest.

The next morning, Singing Wind set out at a fast pace, determined to find a friendly village soon. Turning to the wind spirits, she invoked their power to direct her tattered moccasins on the correct path.

She chose her steps with care, crossing the brush-littered ground—struggling to avoid the thorny cactus. Sagebrush rolled and tumbled silently across the vast grassland. *Keep on moving,* her spirit warned her. *Death will catch you if you stop.*

Several sleeps passed before Singing Wind reached the last of a long line of buttes. She had spent her entire life in the Northern Plains, and she had never seen country like this. Empty land spread before her as far as she could see. Bluffs covered with scraggly pines lay to the north, and multi-colored sandstone buttes jutted against the western sky. To the south lay dry, flat land.

She was hopelessly lost.

FIVE

New Mexico Territory, August 1879

The horses snorted and began prancing when they inhaled the sharp odor of death. Upwind, Lieutenant Jackson and his men couldn't smell it yet. A trained horseman, Jackson loosened his grip on the reins, permitting his mare to continue at her own pace. When the mare reached the narrow neck of the wagon trail, she reared and refused to go farther. Tightening his hold, Jackson drove her forward. She whinnied but obeyed.

"What is it, old girl?" Jackson asked softly, stroking the mare's neck to quiet her fear. He noticed the other men experiencing similar behavior from their mounts. "Company halt!" he shouted over the horses' nervous whickering. He dismounted and sent Barney and the Crow scout, Paloma, up the hill to investigate. They rounded the brushy corridor and crept in.

Moments later, Barney shouted, "Oh, lordy lord! Better come on up here, Lieutenant!"

Jackson handed his reins to his aide and walked up the trail. Upon reaching the battlefield, he saw soldiers' festering, bloated bodies stinking to high heaven.

"Oh God, how horrible!" he said, choking. "How many are there?"

"It's Sergeant Clark and the whole squad," Barney said, "except Bill Mates."

Jackson pulled out his handkerchief and covered his mouth to keep from vomiting. *Thirteen men dead, left to rot. Who could have done this?* He strained to regain his composure, then said, "I'll send a detail to bury them. Barney, you and Paloma continue searching the area and report back to me the number of ambushers."

As the lieutenant walked stoop-shouldered down the road, a great weight seemed to settle upon him. The killing of Clark and his men—so recently confident and full of life—left him acutely aware of his own mortality. A profound sadness filled him at the loss of such young men's lives. His eyes blurred, and he wiped them before issuing the burial orders.

When the soldiers had dug shallow graves and buried the bodies, Jackson read aloud from his leather-bound Bible. The young men stood at attention, while the bugler played "Taps." As the last note of the bugle faded, each man raised his rifle and shot a round into the sky.

"Company dismissed," the lieutenant declared in a shaking voice. The soldiers put their rifles down and rushed to the river for a drink.

"Request permission for chow time?" a young trooper asked smartly.

"Permission granted," the lieutenant answered, wondering how in the world the men could eat at a time like this. The young recruits seemed to have little regard for any life other than their own.

Paloma and Barney returned from the battleground. "With the littering of shells and footprints," Paloma reported, "the killers number no more than seven."

"Only seven?" Jackson asked in disbelief. Paloma remained silent, so he continued, "I want to find out where those murderers went before they attack the settlers around here."

Jackson and Barney accompanied Paloma to the bottom of the hill. "About twenty horses heading north," he said, pointing to the tracks he discovered.

"Seven killers?" Barney recollected. "I bet 'em girls that stole O'Riley's horses and tricked that Mexican trader corralled more redskins to help 'em." He slapped his hand across his forehead. "Yep, no doubt about it. Them damn savage sisters done it again."

Lieutenant Jackson shook his head in disbelief. *No, I just cannot accept that two Indian girls and their companions could have executed this ambush.* He resolved to find the truth, and those damned girls, too.

After days of slow, painstaking tracking, Paloma raised his hand to stop Jackson's platoon. Before him, a multitude of hoofprints blanketed the ground. After sliding off his horse, he found horse track upon horse track completely covering the earth for two hundred paces. The tracks so trampled, the area looked like some kind of stampede must have occurred.

"Barney," he ordered, "circle around these tracks to the east. I'll circle west, and we will meet to the north."

Scanning the mountainside, Paloma spotted a few stray horses, possibly some of those lost in the ambush. He heard Lieutenant Jackson send out a detail to round them up as he began to circle the trampled ground.

Some distance before him, Paloma found straight trails of a mule and two horses, westbound. *Only ridden or led horses would walk in a long, straight line,* he thought, sure that more tracks lay ahead. Several paces to the north, he found a little-used path, leading westward into the Mescalero stronghold in the mountains. Just then, he spotted another two sets of horse prints going the same way. *They killed Clark and his men with only one minor injury, judging from the small stains of blood on the rocks. If they set up another ambush in those steep mountains, these idiot soldiers will get killed, and I will die with them.* Farther on, he saw two more sets and walked forward. He laughed to himself. *A few hundred paces to the west, they will all converge. If Barney finds more tracks, it's best for all of us to let these go unreported.*

"A set of tracks movin' north!" Barney yelled from the east.

Paloma sighed in relief, then looked around and saw Jackson riding in from the south. He kept walking and found three tracks pointing northward. He met up with Jackson and Barney, just north of the maze of prints.

"I counted four sets of horse tracks," Barney said.

"Three on my side," Paloma added, relieved the tracks matched the number of shooters.

"They converge here," Jackson said, "all heading north."

"Them seven scoundrels that ambushed Clark!" Barney exclaimed.

"They ran the horses in circles here to confuse us," Paloma said, "then let them go."

"Why did the Indians leave all these horses behind?"

"Ain't no way a' tellin'," the old codger replied. "All I kin say is the Injuns left 'em here and kept a-goin'."

Jackson had very little faith in Barney, the old drunk who traded Indian stories for free drinks at the fort. Hell, he didn't really trust Paloma either. He cut his eyes at the scout. "Tell me, Paloma, what makes you so sure all the ambushers rode north? It seems to me they ran their horses in circles to give some the chance to split off."

"Look for yourself, sir," Paloma offered, pointing back. "These are the only straight tracks leaving the stampede."

Distrust of his trackers left Jackson with a feeling of dread. *I should do that, circle the area and see for myself. This doesn't add up.* Then, he reconsidered. *These are the only two trackers I have. Even Paloma wouldn't risk the stockade for telling such a bald-faced lie. I'm sure of one thing. If I retrace his steps and find nothing, he'll feel insulted and make himself a thorn in my side. And I guess I wouldn't blame him.*

He swung his head around. "Men, bring whatever horses you found and follow us." He spurred his horse in the ribs and started north.

SIX

New Mexico Territory, September 1879

Golden Eagle stopped his horse along rise that overlooked a sparkling river. Having followed the river's course since daybreak, he chose this as a good place to rest and survey the area. He dismounted and sat in the shade of a cottonwood tree. The glaring rays of the high-noon sun beat down from above. He wiped the sweat from his forehead and fanned at his long hair. It was a beautiful day, unusually hot for early autumn. He had not relaxed like this for many suns and hated to leave the shade.

He heard a noise behind him and jerked his head around. There stood Crossing Wolf and Two Feathers, both worn thin and dirt-caked like himself. He and his companions had gone without food for two sleeps. They could not continue at this pace much longer, and he had no right to expect them to.

The thought of a swim in the cool water made Golden Eagle grin, and he gestured for the others to follow him. The three slowly slipped down the hillside, each man carrying a loaded Springfield rifle in the crook of his arm.

When they reached the river, Crossing Wolf signaled to the others that he had found footprints leading downstream. He crouched down and touched a boot print, then motioned to Golden Eagle to come closer. "Soldiers were here only days ago." He stepped over to another set of tracks. "Indians were here many suns earlier. Unless there is such a thing as moccasin-clad Mexicans."

Golden Eagle raised his eyebrows. "What do you mean?"

"Look over here." Crossing Wolf bent down and picked up a handful of food scraps. "Frijoles, prickly pear cactus, and chili peppers—all Mexican food. Now, look at the footprints. Some people were wearing moccasins."

"Come and see what I have found," Two Feathers called from across the shallow river.

Crossing Wolf waded through the water, then examined the ground carefully. "Many soldiers have been here. They stood here, as we are now. Look at the cigar stubs and their ration sacks."

"Which way did they go?" Golden Eagle asked as he approached.

"It looks as if they came from that old roadway over there and left the same way." Crossing Wolf pointed to a path that led up a hill.

Golden Eagle studied the footprints again, hoping to find conclusive evidence of Thunder. He wondered if she had taken a husband. The thought made him sick.

Looking across the land, he saw how the ground angled upward, then leveled off. All the prints indeed led in that direction, so they agreed to investigate. After reaching the top of the hill, they entered a thicket of trees and brush lining a treacherous corridor.

Crossing Wolf silently halted them.

"What is it?" Golden Eagle asked in a hushed tone.

"Not what, but who," Crossing Wolf answered, pointing to some shells on the ground, next to a bloodstained boulder.

Gripped with an irrational fear that Thunder had shed this blood, Golden Eagle gasped. "No!"

"You do not know whose blood it is," Crossing Wolf hissed.

Golden Eagle banished the unwarranted grief from his mind. He stood and looked around, noticing many saddles strewn randomly at the base of the hill. *Soldiers would not leave those behind. The Indians won the battle, pulled the gear off, and took the horses.* Pointing at the saddles, he said, "Let us walk down for a closer look."

"There are many graves over here," Two Feathers announced from the sandy base of the hill.

They did not need to unearth the occupants from the graves. Their digging sticks probed deeply enough to see that every corpse wore blue.

"I think the Indians ambushed the soldiers," Two Feathers surmised, "then headed north. The big group of soldiers who came a few suns ago must have buried the bodies."

Golden Eagle walked up the hill again to look in the greenery for any signs of Thunder. He returned to the large blood-blackened stone. He crouched down to take a closer look and found a flint arrowhead. *It is the exact design taught by my father! It has to be Thunder's!*

Holding the flint tightly in his fist, he could feel a heartbeat. *She is alive!* He raised his arms in prayer and thanked the Ganhs for protecting her.

"I will find you," he whispered. "I will find you."

SEVEN

Colorado, September 1879

The blue sky turned dark as late afternoon clouds churned. Singing Wind slid down a deep gully, hoping to find shelter. Gnarled tree limbs and other debris covered the dry riverbed at the bottom of a deep gash in the earth. Bellows of thunder grumbled in the distance, and the air grew heavy with moisture. Dry stalks of ocotillo and bitterweed brush bent in the wind.

She ran for cover while watching the rain approach until large drops of water began to spatter her. The cold rain stung her face and arms as she reached the nearest stone outcropping. She carefully stepped over slick limestone and onto a small ledge set into the rock face, sheltered by an overhang. Rain continued to pour from the deep purple sky, and large chunks of ice pelted the ground. Exhausted, she lay down and dozed off.

A roar, sounding like an enormous waterfall, startled her

awake. Alarmed, Singing Wind stood to find the source of the noise. Suddenly a huge wave of water came rushing down the arroyo and into her shelter. Before she could move, the wall of cold water slammed into her body, hurling her backward.

Singing Wind tried to keep her senses while feeling her insides sinking toward her feet. Swallowed by the deluge and swept away, she had no idea what to do. She had to get to the surface for air but could not see anything in the dark, swirling water. Powerless, she scraped repeatedly against something hard and unmoving—*stone walls of the arroyo?* The raging current spat her up to the surface. Inhaling, she took in water with the air as the current pulled her under once more. Resisting the urge to cough, she pulled her eyes tightly shut and grimaced as she held the air in her lungs. *Great Spirit,* she pleaded, *give me a refuge! I beg you!*

Her torso slammed into something, and an explosion of pain lashed into her armpit. She clamped her arms around the object and hugged it for dear life. As her fingers felt a rough surface, she recognized the texture—tree bark! Desperately, she felt along the trunk and discovered a branch under her. She reached out farther and found that the branch angled downward. *No! I am upside down!* Her ribs rebelled in pain as she spun her body over. Barely able to use her battered arm, she managed to thrust herself upward with her uninjured arm and legs.

Finally, her head broke through the surface. She could take only short draughts of air between coughing spasms. Slowly regaining her breath, she spat repeatedly to rid her mouth of grit.

As Singing Wind collected her wits, her body ached from fatigue. Her usable arm could barely hold her body against the current's pull. Straining every muscle, she climbed to an upper limb and sat there.

The flood rose toward her, and she knew she had not escaped yet. The parched earth seemed unable to swallow so much rain in such a short time. The water whipped madly against the sides of the arroyo as it sought every possible outlet. If the water rose much farther, she had no way to climb higher.

Through cold lips, Singing Wind murmured a prayer of gratitude for surviving the flood so far. Then she petitioned the Great Spirit to protect her for another night.

By the next morning, the rain had stopped, and the floodwaters receded. Singing Wind climbed down from the tree with care and examined the wounds under her right arm. Some skin had peeled from her ribcage; she would need to find some medicinal herbs soon.

Walking in the mucky riverbed, Singing Wind saw no trees except the one that had saved her life. Eventually, she emerged from the arroyo to see a breathtaking landscape. The sun shone across the land, creating a beautiful vista of soft prisms as bright sun rays reflected in pools like crystals. The whole countryside had become sparkling, clean, and inviting. She thanked the Great Spirit for letting her live to enjoy this wonderful world.

After cleaning and treating her wounds as best she could, Singing Wind studied the countryside. The tall saguaros had grown swollen with water. As she had learned from childhood stories, the cacti had to store enough water to live through the dry moons. It told her that summer had ended.

Singing Wind had lost everything that she had carried—even her moccasins. She still had her life and wanted to show her gratitude to the Great Spirit. After gathering an armful of sweet grass and silver sage, and placing it carefully on a stone, she offered her sacrifice to the Great Spirit for sparing her life.

Over the next few suns on the move, the land grew uneven. Singing Wind made another knife to replace the one she lost in the flood and, once again, cut sticks for fish traps and twisted yucca leaf strings together to make more snares. Unfortunately, neither caught much food. The climb steepened, and the trees grew thicker. Buzzing insects filled the air. Lacking bear grease or buffalo fat to rub on her skin, she suffered many bites. She scratched the welts on her arms and legs until they bruised and bled.

I am so tired of eating prickly pears and yampa roots, she lamented while shambling toward the nearest pine-covered hill. She did not know what was ahead, but her only hope was to keep moving onward.

On she walked, right through the Moon of Scarlet Plums and into the Season of Falling Leaves. The long journey had taken its toll. Singing Wind limped, weak from hunger and exhaustion. Here, on the vast, rolling landscape, time and place did not exist. Everything seemed the same, except for an occasional chipmunk or raccoon that darted from the brush.

Since her escape from the Pawnee two moons earlier, the days had continually grown shorter, the sun cooler on her back. As the nights grew colder, Singing Wind began to worry. If she did not find a village soon, it would be impossible to survive the winter alone.

EIGHT

New Mexico Territory, September 1879

A buzzard circled over a lone cabin at the base of an enormous sand-colored cliff. Thunder lay alongside Maria in the prairie grass, scrutinizing the farmstead. The shack looked as though the dweller had built part of it inside the mountain. It had to belong to whites. No Indian would live in a place with no route of escape.

A small, dark-haired boy of about ten winters emerged from the cabin and picked up a three-legged stool nearby. A brown-and-white-spotted cow left its grazing and ran directly to him. The boy rubbed and scratched the animal's neck, saying soft words that Thunder could not hear. He seated himself on the stool beside the animal and pulled on her teats. Thunder thought the animal would grow angry at such abuse. The cow, however, stood calmly as white liquid splashed into a bucket that the boy held between his knees.

"How silly the white man's creatures are," Thunder whispered to Maria.

Maria laughed and said, "The boy just wants *leche*."

Thunder motioned for Maria to wait, then crept through the tall grass for a closer look. Watching the boy instead of her footing, she tripped over something. At her feet, a body of a small boy lay face down in the dirt, dead. A single bloody hole gaped in the back of his shirt. His scalp had been cut away, the blood recently dried. *Killed earlier today.* Picking up his rifle, she discovered—to her shock—that she held only a wooden replica, smeared with dark grease. She turned the body over with the fake gun, which revealed him of about eight winters. She was saddened by the senseless killing of this young, harmless boy. *Whoever killed him will kill anybody.* Considering the danger of leaving Maria alone, Thunder returned to her.

The boy finished with the cow, and it wandered back to the field, where a calf waited. As the boy drank from the bucket, milk splashed over his mouth, down his neck, and onto his shirt. When he lowered the pail, he gazed around, then turned toward the cabin. His short-legged pants slapped against his legs as he half-walked, half-ran back to the house.

Thunder suggested they return to camp and inform the others. "We must find out who killed the boy," she advised. "They may come for us."

Back at camp, Thunder told Star and Victoria about all she had seen. Everyone feared the raiders might have remained in the area. If they had left, the group would attack the cabin for goods.

To prepare for a confrontation, and show group solidarity and spirit, they all used Star's collection of paints to adorn each other with their special medicines. Thunder had Star paint the right half of her face black, representing anger or grief, and the other half red for blood, a symbol of strength. Thunder painted Star's face green with white circles: green for all growing things, and the circles for the never-ending circle of life. Victoria and Maria had no medicines of their own, so they painted symbols they liked but held no meaning. Thunder laughed when she saw that Victoria had painted a bright red cross on Maria's nose.

They rode from the campsite, fanning out in search of enemies on their way to the cabin. Circling the homestead in a wide arc, Thunder grew increasingly confident that the raiders had gone. One by one, they reached the cabin, where they formed a semi-circle around its front side.

"Come out with no weapons," Thunder called, "or we will attack."

The cabin door flung open, slamming against the opposite wall. The boy tramped onto the porch. Enraged, he looked Thunder directly in the eye. "What do you want now?"

His venomous question left her tongue-tied. His face radiated fierceness, and his piercing eyes accentuated his belligerent exterior. Finally, she managed to answer, "Food. We're hungry."

The boy's voice growled from deep inside. "You took all the food this morning!"

Confused, Thunder dismounted and jumped onto the porch. "We have not been here before. Get your mother and father. Tell them we'll take food in exchange for their lives."

The boy reached up and seized her hair. With flared nostrils and flattened white lips, he pulled and twisted with all his strength. Thunder grabbed his fists and struggled to break his vise-like grip. As she broke free, she shouted, "Your mother and father! Where are they, boy?"

"They're dead!" he shrieked. "You already killed them!"

"We have never been here before!" Thunder screamed back at him. She pushed him away, aware now that he was mistaking her and her friends for the raiders. "We did not kill your parents!" She let her hands fall to her sides, signaling the fight had ended. She softly asked, "Please, tell me what happened."

The sound of her caring voice seemed to catch the boy off guard. Angrily looking at the women, he said, "The paint on your faces means you're here to kill me."

"Yes, we came ready to fight," Thunder said, "but now we see no need to."

The boy seemed to lose his anger and began to sob. "I was playing guns with my brother this morning and hid from him over there." He pointed to a stand of timber nearby. "While I was on the lookout for Joey to come after me, some Indians came and killed my parents. I stayed hidden, and they didn't see me. Joey never showed up, so I got scared and sneaked into the house."

Thunder assured the boy that he need not be afraid. They would not hurt him. Hesitantly, she told him that she had found his brother, dead. Tears ran down his ashen cheeks, but he stood strong, refusing to wipe his face.

Thunder looked at the newly orphaned boy, frightened and completely alone. He reminded her of the stark horror she had felt after returning to her massacred village. Hatred for the soldiers reignited within her, but this poor boy had brought her no harm. She remembered Snow, fighting Polecat to protect her so long ago. Now, she had a chance to return the favor.

She bent down and hugged the boy. If she made him feel important, he would likely come with them. "Please come with us. We are four women alone. We need a man to take care of us."

The boy stopped sobbing. He stared at them one by one, then whispered, "If you wipe that paint off your faces." Turning and translating his words, Thunder saw the others could hardly keep from smiling.

As Thunder took the boy into the home, she told Star in Cheyenne, "While I keep him busy gathering his things, find the dead and bury them."

Inside the house, Thunder told the boy they would need supplies for the impending winter. "Can we take some blankets," she asked, "winter clothes, and cooking utensils?"

He nodded.

Later, as Thunder and the boy came outside, Victoria suggested they kill the cow and calf for extra meat to dry. When Maria drew her rifle at the cow, however, the boy ran to stop her.

"Do not kill the cow, Maria," Thunder said. "We will find other food." She turned to the boy. "What is your name?"

"John Paul Moore," he said, breathing shallowly.

"Those are too many white people's names for us to remember. Since you are the only man among us, we will call you Brother."

The boy agreed.

"Okay, Brother, can you ride a horse?" Thunder asked as she mounted Stormy.

"I never tried, but I think I can."

Thunder remembered the first time she had ridden Stormy. *If he wets himself, I will need to throw him in a creek.* Reaching down, she pulled him up in front of her. "I will teach you later."

NINE

Colorado, September 1879

Inside Fort Tharp's horse barns, O'Riley stabbed his pitchfork into the deep manure. He thought back to when he had reported to Colonel Edwards two months earlier.

After reading his record, the colonel had stared at him. "Molesting an Indian school girl and massacring an entire Apache village." Edwards carefully returned the papers to the file. "Despicable charges." He shook his head. "However, since you have not been convicted of these allegations, you are ordered to clean the horse barns indefinitely. If you do your job well without complaint, I'll consider a reassignment for you. However, if I hear of one more hint of misconduct, you will be discharged."

As O'Riley unloaded the pitchfork into a manure wagon, he saw PFC, Kaufman, his superior, playing poker with three others. *Every day, the whole day long, leaving me to clean the horse barns alone.* O'Riley's anger simmered. "Bastards," he said through gritted teeth, careful to keep his voice low.

He stabbed the pitchfork back into the edge of the barn's seemingly endless manure. Since he did the work by himself, the detail had fallen behind. A week before, Colonel Edwards had ordered them to stay on the task from dawn to dusk.

O'Riley vehemently dumped another loaded pitchfork into the manure wagon. *Eighteen years in the Army, the first four under General Grant in the War Between the States. Then assigned out west to clear the frontier. Now, grunt work under a lazy private half my age. That Apache girl, Talks Like Thunder, ruined my record. Somehow, I'll figure out a way to get reassigned to Fort Cauley and hunt her down!*

The next day at mid-morning, O'Riley wiped the sweat from his forehead and stabbed his pitchfork into the manure again. Hearing some commotion behind him, he turned and saw Kaufman and his buddies arriving with pitchforks. Right behind them, Corporal Grosland approached.

"Sergeant O'Riley, wash up and report to headquarters," he said. "Colonel Edwards wants to speak with you in ten minutes."

"I'll be there shortly," O'Riley answered, bracing himself for a possible complaint from Kaufman. *If he's trying to further turn Edwards against me, he's bitten off more than he can chew. I'll say my piece before I leave.*

O'Riley hurried to his quarters, washed, slipped on his best uniform, and stood before Colonel Edwards minutes later.

The bald-headed colonel grabbed papers from his desk and

stood, a head taller than O'Riley. "It seems you're not much help in cleaning the horse barns."

"I've done my best, sir," O'Riley flustered, "all by m'self. Kaufman and the others only take up their pitchforks and work when somebody else is watching."

"He claims you're the one distracting his men from work."

O'Riley flushed. "All right, sir, don't take my word for it. Put a man to spy on the barn this afternoon and you'll know fer yourself."

The colonel smiled. "You're right, I don't take your word, considering your record. However, I will give you one more chance on the frontier."

"Yes, sir," O'Riley said. "I'm ready to serve the country by rounding up those redskins."

"I have eight young men to send to the border between Montana Territory and Canada. Sitting Bull has encamped north of the border, and natives are leaving our lands to join his rebels. This is becoming a burden to Canada, and President Hayes requires the Army to stop them. You have the options of either leading a squad of the Montana border patrol or continuing to clean horse barns."

O'Riley knew he had no choice but to go seven hundred miles farther from the southwest. "I'm ready to lead the border patrol, sir."

O'Riley noticed the colonel staring at the side of his face. "That girl you brawled with sure got the best of you. God, that's one damned ugly scar."

Furious, O'Riley felt the blood rising to this face but managed to stay quiet.

"I have told the men to alert me if you break any regulations. Control yourself."

"Yes, sir." O'Riley saluted and left headquarters. *Border patrol ain't much better than cleaning barns—riding all day for months on end, baked in long summer days and shivering in frigid winters. No chance of getting back to the southwest.* "One damned ugly scar" ran through his mind. *That little squaw, Talks Like Thunder, has made my life hell.*

TEN

New Mexico Territory, September 1879

"We followed those seven trails north for days, but the ground turned to solid rock," Lieutenant Jackson reported. "We searched north of there for miles, but the tracks never reappeared. With no trail to follow, I thought it best to return to the fort." Jackson paused, then concluded, "My men and I are worn thin, and we were too short of supplies to ride into the northern territory. I thought it best to come back here for new orders, sir."

Captain Baker bolted up from his chair. "New orders, hell! I want those Indian girls caught! I can believe they killed Clark and twelve other men in an ambush. What I *can't* believe is that a lieutenant and an entire platoon of twenty trained men can't find them."

"You don't really believe those girls are responsible for killing Clark's squad, do you?"

"Of course, I do. Bill Mates was there. In fact, he claims he wounded an Apache girl before running for his life."

Jackson shook his head. "It's just not conceivable that girls could outsmart Clark and his men."

Captain Baker moved to within three inches of Jackson's face. "I don't know why. It looks like they've outsmarted you and yours!"

The lieutenant's face grew red with anger, and his jaw clamped tightly shut.

"You should have brought ol' Barney here," the captain continued. "I'd like to know what he has to say for himself."

The lieutenant looked at the captain. "Sir, Paloma claims there were seven shooters. Maybe those girls joined up with other Indians."

Growing calmer, the captain returned to his desk. "I'm certain the same two girls are behind all these attacks. Regardless, bring them in. Then we'll know."

"Sir, if we can get enough food and ammunition, we'll go back."

"Prepare to leave first thing tomorrow morning."

"Yes, sir."

"I'll see to your supplies. I want an end to these killings, and I'll have it. Do you think thirty men will be enough to catch them, or do you think you will need more?"

No answer came, nor had Baker expected one. After a crisp salute, Lieutenant Jackson turned and left.

The next day, Jackson's men rose before reveille. Barney, Paloma, and four others were the only seasoned veterans to ride with their lieutenant; the other twenty-four men were recent recruits. Jackson looked them over and rubbed his head as if he could already feel the pain coming. "Move out!" he yelled.

Days later, after they entered the mountains, the tension began building. The young men's fear of closing in on the cunning savage sisters caused them to jump at every jackrabbit and covey of quail taking flight.

Each night as they camped, the veterans sat around the campfire, spinning tales of battles they had fought against Indians. With straight faces, they concocted imaginary horrors of blood and mayhem, then sat back and watched the boys recoil in awe and fear.

One night, Barney sat nearby, thinking aloud. "Hope we don't run across any 'pache war parties. These here boys'd most likely mess their britches and run." He kept his voice low, not wanting Paloma to hear him. "An Injun's an Injun, an' I don't trust none of 'em."

Later, after everyone had bedded down, two recruits continued to talk in the dark.

"I don't know how you feel, Billy, but I don't much like the idea of hunting girls."

"And pretty girls, if you can believe that fat, old Mexican fart, Sanchez."

"I know. Do you think you'll be able to shoot them?"

"Depends. If they're shooting at me, then I guess I can shoot at them."

"Yeah, you're right, only I still don't like it."

"Go to sleep!" the lieutenant shouted through the darkness. "I'm tired of hearing about those damned girls!"

Barney remained quiet for a change, busily scratching the nits on his head. *How'd I get m'self in this fix? I shouldn'a been braggin' 'bout knowin' so much. Lord's the onlyist one that knows what 'em blame savages is apt to do. I done stayed alive this long by mindin' my own business, and I figger it's plum stupid to change. Soon as I've a chance, I'm a-gettin' m'self back to the fort.*

Paloma sat alone, watching and listening. He sensed that Barney and the lieutenant did not trust him. He served as a scout for only one reason: money for his family. A long time earlier, he had decided that the whites would inevitably defeat the outnumbered Indians. He didn't really care about the war anymore. His own tribe had lost many when conquered early on, and he hated the army that he served.

Paloma looked across at Barney and smiled. *That old man couldn't find his behind with both hands...I can warn those Apache girls, if they're out there.* He got to his feet and put another log on the fire, aware such high flames could be seen for miles.

When not a single soldier objected, a sly smile spread across his face. His evil laugh echoed through the camp as he walked from the raging blaze.

ELEVEN

Colorado, October 1879

In the Season of Falling Leaves, Thunder's group made camp in the mountains between the North Platte and Arkansas Rivers. To the west, the Rocky Mountains rose in a towering wall of unbroken stone. This secluded location had ample food and water. Compared to the other places they had camped during the last moon of travel, it was an ideal campsite.

"I just told the others that we will camp here for the winter," Thunder told Star at the river while scrubbing her face with a wet piece of leather.

Star locked her eyes on Thunder. "Why?" she exclaimed, then sat with her mouth agape.

"Are you upset?"

"You know I want to find the Cheyenne. We could travel two more moons before winter."

Thunder shook her head. "I know how important it is for you to bring your bundle to the Cheyenne. I apologize."

"Then why," Star asked gently, "do you want to winter here?"

Thunder said nothing for a moment and appeared to withdraw into herself. Finally, she said, "I have to."

Star realized a crushing burden consumed Thunder. "What is it?"

"I did not know how to tell you, so I've kept it to myself for many days."

"Kept what to yourself?"

"And I hoped it would not come to pass..." Thunder seemed to speak to her inner shadows of worry and self-recrimination.

"Thunder," Star implored, "please tell me what weighs on your heart. You do not need to bear it alone."

Thunder looked down and mumbled, "I am carrying the trapper's baby."

Star stayed silent for a long moment. *Thunder could have told me any time in the last few moons. It was my fault. She was afraid of how I would react.* She sighed, admitting to herself that Thunder had chosen wisely to give birth in this place.

Few words seemed right, but Star finally managed, "How can I help you?"

"Do not stop me from killing it the moment it leaves my body!"

The outburst shocked Star into silence. A moment later, Thunder continued more quietly, "If you carried the trapper's baby, would you not kill it too?"

"No," Star whispered. "I feel the spirits have a purpose for this child. Search your heart and listen to your spirit."

"I will not bother to do that."

Deeply saddened, Star took a deep breath to compose herself.

"Remember, sister, I share the responsibility for your pregnancy. I will help you with raising your baby as much as I can."

"Do not worry. You will not need to."

Star fought off the urge to respond harshly and quelled her own mounting anger. Without another word, she went back to camp and rearranged her mind and her things for a long stay.

After their midday meal, Thunder told everyone they needed to prepare for the coming cold weather. Eventually, the group agreed to build a lodge.

First, they would need an axe to cut poles to the proper size. Thunder found an excellent stone, which everyone took turns chipping into an axe head. While the others worked, Star scoured the area for the biggest yucca plants. She pounded and washed the fibers. After they dried, she wound them into rope for binding the poles together. Once the group had chopped the poles to equal length, Thunder marked a large circle on the ground. Everyone else helped her dig holes two paces apart around the circle, then erected sixteen poles, one in each hole. Next, they bent the pole tops together and tied them with strands of yucca to form high, inward-curving walls. Finally, they lashed more poles straight across the top to make a strong roof. The structure was similar to a tipi but much stronger.

After completing the framework, Thunder showed the others how to cover it with a thatching of bear grass. Victoria amazed everyone by improving the lodge's design. Often stopping for breath, she added layers of sod around the lodge, then sealed them with mud. An opening remained at the top of the lodge to allow smoke to escape the otherwise airtight structure.

Thunder and Brother covered the ground inside with a thick layer of sweetgrass. From the supplies they brought out blankets, some from Brother's house and others taken from the soldiers after the ambush. They laid blankets over the sweetgrass to make comfortable bedding and still had some left to cover themselves.

While the two worked on the interior, the others started building a smaller lodge for cooking and storage.

During the next two moons they collected nuts, berries, and plants—everything they could find. They set snares, catching small game, and Thunder brought back meat from hunts. However, the meat they preserved would not hold out for more than a half-moon, and besides the food, they needed large, thick animal pelts for blankets and winter clothing. Her pregnancy would soon make it too awkward for her search for game.

Hunting works against Star's nature and medicine power, so I cannot expect her to kill for the band. Maria has improved with a rifle and shows enthusiasm for hunting. But the whole cold season will pass before she develops the patience and silence needed for finding game. Long before winter's end, we will be cold and hungry, without a hunter.

Star told everyone snow would soon cover the ground throughout the cold season, leaving the horses nothing to eat. So, the group gathered dried grass and many different types of tree bark for the animals. Thunder was sure they would need a shelter from the wind, so she cut young trees to build a wall. As the others completed their work, they helped her. Before long, the windbreak was large enough for all the horses.

Pleased they had completed their winter preparations in time, they celebrated by holding an outdoor feast. At the end of the meal,

Thunder noticed Brother had not eaten much. He had grown thin. Over the last moon he had worked half-heartedly, often leaving tasks unfinished. Many nights he would awaken screaming, then settle into tears and sobs. Other than tending the fire, no activity seemed to bring him contentment.

Thunder watched him gazing into the campfire with sad eyes, his mind seemingly in another world. "We know you miss your family, Brother."

Brother swallowed hard, gasped for air, and wailed. He cried for a long time. No one touched him or said a word. They let him stay in his grief as long as he needed.

His sobbing stopped, but he did not look up from the ground.

Thunder moved over and put her hand on his shoulder. "You have a new life and new friends now. In time, the pain will lessen."

Brother nodded. He took from his pocket a fire flint that Thunder had given him and rolled it in his hands. Smiling, Maria jumped up and swiped the flint from him.

"Gimme that back, you dumb ol' girl!" he shouted. In a whirlwind of motion, he charged the laughing girl, punching and kicking at the same time.

"That's enough out of you two. Stop or I'll..." Victoria threatened.

"Okay, here it is," Maria said, giggling. She held out her open hand.

Everyone's laughter seemed to help break the despondent mood.

As the women chattered, Brother sat in silence, again glumly tossing and rubbing his flint. Before long, he leaned back against a large rock and fell asleep.

Victoria carried him into the lodge and took a few moments to catch her breath. With the tenderness of a mother, she covered the boy with his blanket and bent to kiss his cheek. "I never thought I would speak to a *gringo*," she whispered, in awe, "and here I am kissing one."

Later, Victoria lay awake thinking about the life she and Maria had found for themselves. A vision of her tiny village of Galeana slipped into her mind. Although she felt homesick, she loved this way of life more than almost anything else. She felt free, really free. Indians never seemed to plan anything; they had no schedule of any kind. Events just seemed to happen. They never hurried, except on a raid. Sometimes she worried, especially about Maria not going to church or school. On the other hand, Maria was learning the most important lesson of her life: self-defense. Victoria was certain that no man would ever enslave Maria again. No, at fifteen, she could ride a horse and shoot a gun as well as any *vaquero*. Thanks to Thunder's training, Maria could now survive anywhere, under any conditions.

Victoria's thoughts turned to the Indian girls. Now, she saw them as anything but savages. True, they did not have a chapel or a *Padre* for religious guidance, but they lived very spiritual lives. They communed with their Great Spirit every day and honored the Creator and all living things in their own way. Victoria also liked the respect that the girls showed her. As she had been born into the lower class in Mexico, few people had ever respected her before.

Still, worries marred Victoria's happiness. Her shortness of breath would make it difficult for her to survive the winter. She feared higher altitude and harsher cold farther north would take her life. She had to tell Maria soon. With that thought in mind, Victoria rolled over, pulled her blanket over her shoulders, and drifted to sleep.

Maria awoke at sunrise and began cooking the morning meal. Wrapped in her warm robe, she smiled. She hung a pot of soup on the spit over the flames and marveled at her present circumstances. She could not remember ever feeling happiness such as she felt now. After living with Thunder for several weeks, she felt as if she had found a big sister. Star had also taught her much, with her growing command of Spanish. Even in Brother, she'd found a brother in every way but blood. She'd never expected to truly have a family but now couldn't imagine life without them. She worked diligently, proud to serve her new clan.

Victoria exited the lodge and approached her.

"Can I help, Maria?" she asked, smiling.

"Sure, add some wood to the fire." Maria put a pot of water over the flames. "Isn't life here wonderful?" She began to stir the pot of soup.

"Yes, we've been blessed here so far." Victoria paused, then grew serious. "But for how long will we stay blessed?"

Maria stopped stirring and turned to face her. "Is the cold making you weak?"

"Yes, that and the thin air leaves me short of breath."

Sensing where her mother was leading the conversation, Maria grew uneasy. "Does that mean you can't survive the winter here?"

"No, I wish to stay here until the weather grows warmer. However, Star has told us about her land. For months, the air turns terribly cold, creating ice so thick that people can walk over rivers and lakes. The wind blows so hard that snow piles deeper than our own height. We would be miserable."

"You think we should go back to Mexico, don't you?"

"In the spring, we should return home."

Maria contemplated leaving her new family, and her heart sank. "*You* should go, Mother, for your health, but I want to remain with Thunder and Star."

Victoria chose her next words carefully. "I'm sure they would try to include you in their lives. But you cannot have a rich, fulfilled life under these circumstances. You know as well as I that the whites will one day take all the tribal land for themselves. Our friends cannot offer you a safe enough place for you to raise a family."

"But Thunder and Star are my family now." Maria looked away, hiding a glare, and resumed stirring the forgotten breakfast.

"You also have a big family in Galeana—cousins, aunts, and uncles."

"I'm not leaving my friends to live with strangers!" Maria swirled the spoon so forcefully that the soup sloshed over the rim.

Victoria stood and calmly said, "We need more wood for the fire. I'll get some."

Watching her mother straining for breath as she slowly walked away, Maria felt ashamed. She smiled sadly, realizing, *Mother needs me to take her home.*

TWELVE

Colorado, November 1879

For thirty days and nights, Lieutenant Jackson's patrol wandered around the remaining tribal hunting grounds. Never did they see even a single Indian, much less a war party led by two girls.

The lieutenant rose at sunrise, hungry and shivering from the cold. Fatigue had taken its toll on morale, as had the chill of riding through many mid-autumn downpours. Famished and disheartened, the men just wanted to go back to the fort.

Looking through his journal, Jackson noticed the date: November 10. Conditions would only get worse. He decided to ride out for Cedar City, five miles away, and telegraph Fort Cauley for permission to return. The men, he knew, dared not hope for recall, but only for fresh food rations. Jackson's own higher hope prompted him to order his troops to clean their uniforms. If he brought them the news he wanted, he wouldn't return to Fort

Cauley leading a slovenly group of men. His superiors would regard him poorly enough for returning empty-handed.

After Jackson's ride to Cedar City and the wait for the responding telegram, he returned to camp at mid-afternoon bearing news better than food.

"We'll start for the fort in the morning," he announced.

After the soldiers' spontaneous cheer, Jackson added, "Baker's telegraph said he had no reports of killer girls in the area. However, he said, and I quote, 'You might consider yourselves lucky those girls didn't find you.'"

The men were not amused. One of the new recruits called out, "Shucks, Lieutenant, you know if our supplies wasn't running out, we would have caught them."

The lieutenant smiled, wondering how his men could have caught the girls when they couldn't even find them. Perhaps his platoon really had been lucky. At least the captain had not needed to send someone to look for them.

THIRTEEN

Colorado, November 1879

Autumn covered the land. A strong sun shone yellow-orange through the nearly bare trees, signifying the end of the Season of Falling Leaves. The raspberry bushes hung full, ready for picking. The palm-wide leaves of oak and hickory had already surrendered and lay dead under active forest feet, bringing forth mind-sharpening smells of decay.

Thunder, having filled her berry baskets late in the afternoon, sat on a large flat rock and began snacking. A moment later, Star came to sit beside her. They exchanged only a soft greeting before sitting silently, observing the changing colors of the hills. A bitter gust of wind came up unexpectedly, and Star swung herself around to shield Thunder.

"You mustn't get chilled, sister. It could be dangerous in your condition."

Thunder was too busy munching berries to answer. She opened her purple-stained mouth and filled it with another handful of the sweet-tart berries.

"Thunder," Star said, "my feeling has grown stronger that the baby you carry is special."

A cold expression of loathing chased the tranquility from Thunder's dark eyes. "I care nothing for what your spirit says about me, Star. I will not change my mind."

Seeing her anguish, Star hesitated, but continued. "I am certain the baby is special and will bring great meaning to your life."

Another gust of cold wind reached down and lifted a mass of red and gold leaves. "Just leave me alone!" Thunder demanded.

The leaves swirled upward, then fell back like silent footsteps on the earth. Star reached into the basket, took a raspberry, and popped it in her mouth. "I am going to help prepare our evening meal."

Detecting a movement, Thunder shaded her eyes with her hand and squinted at the wooded glen below. "Wait!" she cried. "I see someone walking along an animal trail."

"It must be Victoria or Maria."

"I cannot tell. The person is too far away."

Star stooped and picked up the largest leaf she could find. She rolled the leaf into a tube against the palm of her hand and held it up to her right eye. Squeezing her left eye shut, she found the figure coming toward them.

"What are you doing with the leaf?" Thunder asked, curious.

"Do you not know when you look through a tiny opening like this, it blocks out everything around it? It makes the object you see through it look bigger."

"No," Thunder answered, amazed. "I have never heard of such a thing."

"Look," Star offered, handing the coiled leaf to her.

After looking for herself, Thunder agreed. "It is a girl," she said.

"Are you sure it is not Maria?"

"It is not her."

"It must be a stranger. Keep her in sight while I get guns." She left for camp.

Upon returning, Star tossed Thunder the rifle, then she sped down the slope toward the girl but stopped short. The stranger wore a tattered dress, her face looking down, gaunt from starvation.

Star cocked her pistol, then spoke loudly, trying her best to sound big and tough like Thunder. "Who is the foolish one who walks this land without permission?"

The girl stopped and looked up vacantly. Star asked again in Sioux, lowered the gun, and stepped closer. The girl trembled and collapsed onto the ground. Star dropped the pistol, rushed to her, and grabbed her limp body. "Singing Wind," the girl whispered, then passed out.

Great Spirit, we are sisters! "Thunder!" Star yelled. "Tell Maria and Brother to come and help me bring this girl to camp."

The three of them carried Singing Wind into the lodge and laid her on a blanket. Star watched over her and fed her soup broth when she awoke briefly from time to time. Just before dark, Singing Wind had gained enough strength to sit up and eat some stew.

When Victoria, Maria, and Brother returned laden with firewood, Star told them Singing Wind had just begun eating. They sat, anxiously waiting for their guest to finish her meal.

Star introduced Singing Wind to everyone and asked the newcomer why she was traveling so far from home. Singing Wind told her story with as much detail as any good storyteller would, while Star translated Sioux into Apache for Thunder. Next, Thunder translated into English for Brother, and into Spanish for Victoria and Maria. Requiring a pause for translation after every sentence, the story seemed to take forever.

Singing Wind began with her earlier life. Two winters back, her father had been killed in a tribal skirmish. From then on, helping her mother consumed her life until the Pawnee attack. Brother sat wide-eyed as she related her daring escape. Everyone felt wretched when they learned the fate of Singing Wind's friends, Blue Snow and Blackberry.

When Star invited Singing Wind to stay with them, she accepted without hesitation.

Every person in the group had lost home and family—perhaps that was what bound them so tightly together. They voted unanimously to stay together for the winter, but come the Flowering Moon, they would go their separate ways. The nearness of Thunder's time made the decision easy.

They did not crawl into their beds until nearly dawn. Exhausted, Singing Wind fell asleep before anyone else. New friends and a belly full of Star's stew brought her sound sleep for the first time in three moons.

FOURTEEN

Colorado, November 1879

The cedar tree was about four hundred years old. The ground beneath it was warmer and more fragrant than anywhere else in the forest. Within the tree's protective circle, dazzling splashes of light filtered through the heavy limbs onto three sleeping Apaches. The rest of its great boughs obscured the outside world.

The shrill sound of an Army trumpet instantly woke Golden Eagle. Silently, he roused the others, alerting them to the danger they faced. He could not believe they had become so careless as to sleep before scouting the surrounding area. Eight moons of relentless searching for Thunder had left them all so weary. *Perhaps Crossing Wolf and Two Feathers are too tired to continue looking*, he thought. *So much is against us. How much longer can I expect them to help me? Soldiers are everywhere, and rain obliterating all hope of Thunder's trail.*

The three braves crawled from their nest on their bellies so silently that a perched hawk overhead did not stir or squawk a warning. At the edge of a nearby cliff, the Apaches looked down to see a military camp astir. The soldiers seemed to be preparing for departure. Most were packing their things into saddlebags, but a few had already mounted on horses facing the southward trail.

Just as the Apaches had situated themselves comfortably, Two Feathers motioned that they should leave. Golden Eagle held up his hand, indicating for him to wait. "Stay still," he said, no more loudly than the twitching of his lips. "Assess the men, horses, and weapons; then we will plan."

Crossing Wolf whipped his head around, his wide mouth changing from gentleness to firmness with bewildering speed. "Take a good look at the soldiers and tell me what you see."

Golden Eagle looked below with a skeptical eye. "What are you seeing that I am not, brother?"

Crossing Wolf focused on their foes. "Ambush!"

"Ambush." Two Feathers curled his lip with indignation. "We are only three. How can we ambush all those soldiers?"

"They are heading south and have to pass through the canyon we crossed yesterday. If we hide in the cliffs above, we could pick them off like rabbits."

Golden Eagle grinned. "It is a good plan, brother. Think of the many souls we can free. We must ride swiftly to get there before they do."

Crossing Wolf nodded. They slithered back to their horses and maneuvered them cautiously out of the soldiers' earshot. Then they rode as if wolves nipped at their heels.

Upon reaching the canyon, they hid their horses in a nearby ravine. A strong, cold breeze whipped across their faces when they reached the site for the ambush. With rapt attention, they painted one another's faces for battle. Each ended the ritual by singing his own medicine prayer.

Prepared for the upcoming fight, the three Apaches went to the canyon's edge and watched for soldiers.

When a line of horses began to appear in the distance, Crossing Wolf urgently reminded the others, "Remember, you hold the vengeance of our grandfathers in your hands. Their spirits cry out for retribution, and they will be with you. They will strengthen your arm and harden your heart, so you can kill without mercy. If you let one man survive, you will be inviting him back to kill more Apache women and children."

Crossing Wolf hid in the rocks above the far end of the canyon. Two Feathers positioned himself in the middle, and Golden Eagle stepped into a vine-covered crevice near the mouth.

Golden Eagle heard the soldiers speaking in the distance and shook his head in disbelief. *Do they not know death can follow any careless noise?* When they first entered the canyon, apprehension caused him to hold his breath.

As the Bluecoats drew closer, Golden Eagle studied them intently. From his time laboring at the fort, he recognized a lieutenant's markings on the sleeve of the lead rider. Behind him rode an Indian scout and a scrawny frontiersman wearing a floppy brown hat. Following them, riding four abreast, came the soldiers in their dark blue uniforms, their caps sitting cockily on their heads. Shiny gold buttons flashed like gems in the sunlight. Each man wore a pistol on one side and a saber on the other. Sheathed carbines hung from their saddles.

The lieutenant sat on his horse with the expertise of a veteran. The stark whiteness of his skin shone brightly, and he wore a broad, egotistical smile. Unusually tall and as thin as a willow branch, he gave forth an air of assurance and control. Golden Eagle sensed this man had traveled far and witnessed much. With great effort, he forced his eyes away and glanced toward Crossing Wolf.

Gesturing caution, Crossing Wolf signed for them to hold their fire until every soldier had passed Golden Eagle. *Impatient Two Feathers*, Crossing Wolf surmised, *hates watching the easy targets passing beneath him.*

When the last soldiers entered the canyon, the lieutenant suddenly stood on his stirrups and turned backward, glaring. His features contorted, almost as if he sensed the ambush, while Crossing Wolf had him centered in the crosshairs of his Springfield.

Golden Eagle picked off a man in the final row, nearest the canyon mouth.

When the lieutenant saw the man hit, his face froze in stark horror. Crossing Wolf fired. The bullet ripped through his chest, and he fell.

Looking for another target, Crossing Wolf spotted the frontiersman spur his horse's flanks. The animal did not budge until its rider leaped off, then it ran in blind terror. The frontiersman, flat against the ground, snaked toward the canyon wall until Crossing Wolf shot him in the back.

Loading his gun, Crossing Wolf watched the Indian scout slide from his bareback roan. The scout dashed toward the opposite side of the canyon, but Two Feathers shot him mid-stride.

Mass confusion reigned on the canyon floor. The soldiers shook as they aimed their weapons; they seemed to lack the will to fight. As the Apaches pumped shells at anything that moved, the gun smoke formed a thick blue haze that drifted out the mouth of the canyon. When they stopped firing, thirty-one corpses littered the canyon floor. The silence became as empty and depressing as a widow's grief.

At Crossing Wolf's nod, the Apaches left their hiding places and cautiously walked down to count coup on the dead. They entered the dark shadows of the canyon and stood among the fallen without speaking. On the cliff, they had proudly fought for the spirits of their loved ones. Now they saw only dead boys of unshaped youth, devoid of warrior hardiness. They took no scalps or souvenirs. They counted no coup. The warriors felt no pride in having fought this battle. Because of their sore need, they took some of the soldiers' weapons and ammunition.

Golden Eagle felt old, tired, and beaten. He and his friends were no better than the whites who had massacred their women and children.

Why, he wondered, *when there are so many white-eyes, did they send boys to fight a man's battle?*

FIFTEEN

Colorado, November 1879

At dawn, James Carnett beat on the back door of the saloon, knowing that the bartender, Stumpy, slept there. He continued pounding until he heard a sleepy grumble through the door.

"By damn, this better be important, or I'll have yer hide decoratin' my barroom wall."

"It's important, all right!" Carnett yelled. "Gimme a drink to calm my nerves, and I'll tell you what I saw."

A noise of hawking, then spitting, came through the door. "What the hell's wrong?" Stumpy asked in a low growl. "What ya waking me up this time a day fer?" The heavy wooden door swung open, revealing Stumpy in dirty pants held up by red suspenders.

"It's awful, man!" Carnett said, pushing his way into the darkened hallway. "What I saw was just gawd-awful."

"Now tell me what all this hooray and hell-raisin' is about."

"Injuns, man!" Carnett said as the two men surged through the dim corridor leading to the barroom. "That's what it's about. Musta been a pack of them red devils. They done killed a whole passel of soldiers out in Cedar Canyon."

"Oh my gawd!"

The early morning, sunlight had just begun to filter through the dust-covered windows. Stumpy went behind the bar and filled two glasses with rye whiskey, setting one in front of Carnett.

Taking a swig of his drink, Carnett said, "Some of them contrary longhorns we let graze wandered into Cedar Canyon. This morning we went to round 'em up, but low and behold, there they was. Thirty-one soldiers deader'n doornails, the lieutenant and all! I come a-runnin' fast as I could."

"Oh my gawd!" Stumpy kicked back his whiskey.

"Cain't you say nothin' more'n 'Oh my gawd'?"

"Lord help us," Stumpy countered.

"If'n you're needin' help," Carnett said, "you'd better be callin' on somebody a little closer, 'cause them redskins is headin' this way." He finished his drink and slammed the glass down.

"By damn, you ain't a-thinkin' they'd attack this here town, are ya?"

"Can't rightly say. I saw some horse tracks on the prairie. Just figured they was most likely coming over here."

Stumpy stood without a sound, apparently ruminating on the news. "Let's have another drink," he finally said as he filled both glasses again.

Carnett downed his glass in a few quick swallows, and Stumpy did the same. As the two men walked out the saloon door, Stumpy said, "I'll go find the sheriff, and you start wakin' folks up."

Within the hour, Captain Baker was seated at his dining room table rereading the scrap of paper in his hand. *Surely,* he thought, *there must have been some mistake. How could Lieutenant Jackson and all his men be dead? For months, no incidents had been reported of Indians jumping the reservations. It's too cold for an Indian attack that powerful.* He shook his head and read the telegram once more.

Before eight, the captain left Fort Cauley with fifty capable men. They traveled light, with only guns and ammunition, and reached Cedar City in four and a half hours.

Built on an open plain sandwiched between mountains, Cedar City provided visibility over a great distance. Baker thought they'd easily see a war party long before it could get close enough to attack.

Other than a squad of lookouts at the edge of the deathly quiet town, not a single person was outside. Baker's men rode down the middle of Main Street and stopped in front of the sheriff's office. The jailhouse door swung open and out walked Colonel Bill Edwards and Sheriff Johns. Edwards, Baker realized, must have arrived earlier and posted the lookouts.

After a salute and a couple of handshakes, Baker accompanied them into the jail. Over cups of strong, scalding coffee, the three sketched battle plans. Edwards gave orders, and his men took designated places on the north side of the town. Baker stationed his soldiers to the south.

Two young farmers, unaware of any problem, came hauling their goods into town. Soldiers temporarily confiscated their wagons, which Sheriff Johns stationed in front of the hotel. The drivers, concerned for their merchandise, hid inside their wagons.

The owner and the clerk of the town's only mercantile store hid on the building's roof. Exposed to the cold, they nonetheless commanded a view of the entire countryside.

The bank manager waited behind locked doors, a loaded handgun on his desk. Trained soldiers protected his wife and son. He didn't consider himself a coward, but why risk his life needlessly? He had no intention of fighting unless the savages broke in on him.

The sheriff and several businessmen who stood to lose the most money hid among the shadows between the clapboard buildings. Stumpy, the bartender, stayed behind his bar. Some men wanted to die with their boots on, but Stumpy preferred to die tending bar. Actually, he didn't want to die at all. He had done a bang-up good business all morning, much better than usual. Most of the men seemed to need whiskey to build their courage.

The townsfolk waited.

At two-thirty, Baker still stood aiming his Sharps .50-caliber rifle out of the loft of the livery stable. For the hundredth time he tested his sights, allowing for windage and extreme distance. The long-range rifle reminded him of his early days as a top marksman. He wondered how accurately he could shoot now, but no target appeared. So, as planned, he emerged from the stable and sought out the colonel.

Edwards stood with the sheriff outside the jailhouse, both suffering from an acute case of embarrassment. Baker joined them, and the three reconvened inside. After a long and heated discussion, they came to an agreement. Colonel Edwards' troops would remain on guard while Captain Baker and his men rode out and scouted the area. If Baker's men found no evidence of an approaching war party, they would go on to the canyon and investigate.

All the townsmen but the preacher congregated at Stumpy's Saloon, where they consumed several bottles of whiskey and rehashed adventures of Indian battles they had fought. Stumpy, who had to stay sober, silently questioned their unquestionable courage. He figured most of the yarns should be taken with a dose of salt.

By late afternoon, everyone throughout the town could hear the men's drunken singing:

> Rye whiskey, rye whiskey, I'll tell you no lie,
> We'll be drinking rye whiskey 'till the day we die.

Deloris Del Gato, the proprietor of the House of Pleasure, hurried her ladies to bathe and get fixed up. She knew the townsmen would place a big demand on their services that evening. As luck would have it, the first gentlemen were already knocking on the door, even before suppertime.

Captain Baker spread his men sixteen wide as they rode across the flat land toward Cedar Canyon. But no amount of searching turned up even one old hoof print.

An hour before sundown, they reached the canyon entrance and rode in slowly. After the shock of seeing the bodies wore off,

Captain Baker studied the dead men and the surrounding stone walls. Something about the assault struck him as odd. After a moment, it registered: no one had scalped or mutilated the soldiers.

Studying the lay of the bodies, Baker figured ambushers had fired at them from above. He ordered five men to recover any identification or personal belongings, and he directed the others to dig graves. He and his Crow scout climbed up the sandstone cliffs to confirm his assessment of the attack.

"Three shooters," the scout said conclusively.

The captain shook his head. "How could three fighters kill thirty-one men?" He kicked away some discharged shells. "What could Jackson have been thinking?"

"Hard to say, sir," the scout offered. "It's late in the year for this kind of thing. Could be he just was not expecting trouble."

Baker nodded absentmindedly, his thoughts on a couple of girls named Talks Like Thunder and Falling Star. "No, that's crazy," he mumbled.

"What did you say, sir?"

"Nothing, nothing at all."

SIXTEEN

Fort Tharp Colorado, November 1879

Thanksgiving came and went almost unnoticed. For the most part, soldiers sat around the fires in their barracks. Many considered themselves lucky to have enough to eat, but some complained, wanting warmer clothing and better living quarters.

However, on the first day of December, a dispatch came through. Colonel Bill Edwards reread the new orders from Washington: "You are to search out and destroy all the Indian camps in the area."

After the embarrassment in Cedar City, Edwards saw his chance to save face. He ordered in the best soldiers from all the surrounding forts under his command, and from those, he culled the very best. His final selections he made with care, choosing those whom he had personally trained as efficient killing machines. The men cleaned and oiled their rifles, filled their packs with ammunition, and filed their sabers to a razor edge.

Within three weeks, Edwards and his men destroyed every Arapaho, Sioux, and Cheyenne village within a hundred-mile radius. Their collected scalps and souvenirs hung heavily on their horses when they returned from their victories.

Not even this satisfied the colonel. "Men," he lectured, "this war will not end until we capture or kill an old Cheyenne chief named White Blade. I am told he's on the run, with more than a hundred warriors traveling in his band."

SEVENTEEN

Colorado, December 1879

Ghost Face had arrived! He came blowing his frozen breath through every valley and across every mountaintop, daring anyone on the high plains to challenge him.

Singing Wind learned from Thunder that the group desperately needed a hunter. Honored to have skills to offer the others, she enthusiastically took on the challenge. Thunder provided her with a bow and arrows to start hunting right away. As she knew nothing of guns, Thunder taught her how to use the pistols and rifles to hunt with when she mastered them.

All in the camp worked from dawn to dusk.

Victoria and Maria told everyone they planned to depart in spring and go to Yellow Dog's village. There, they would ask the Mescaleros for help to find their way to Galeana. It saddened the group that their friends would be leaving, but they understood what might happen to Victoria if they did not.

Star—always the healer—continued making medicines with the plants she harvested. Victoria worked with her when she could, eager to learn how to use them.

Thunder and Maria stayed in the camp to prepare food and spent their free time preserving meat with dried plants and roots they had collected on their journey.

Star gave them some dried sweet-pea-like blossoms from her herb pouch. They boiled the blossoms and made everyone's favorite flavor of tea. The two girls worked hard, adding nuts and dried berries to several different types of meats, then pounding the mixture into pemmican. When dried, it would keep until the berries came again.

Singing Wind proved herself to be an excellent hunter and a valuable asset to their group. She brought in a kill regularly, then dressed the animal and helped with food preparation. Although capable of cooking almost anything, she specialized in making acorn cakes. After shelling the acorns, she ground them on a flat stone and mixed them with water and berries. She poured the batter on large leaves and laid them in her rock-lined fire hole. The resulting cakes took a lot of work, but everyone found them delicious.

Star excelled in her stew. She could turn their preserved stores of meat, roots and wild vegetables into a mouth-watering meal. The others knew she used herbs, but no amount of heckling would make her reveal the secret ingredients.

Victoria won her fame by making delicious meals from almost nothing. Many times, she would cook only one rabbit coupled with the dried provisions to feed the entire group. The others never knew exactly what went into her meals, but they always turned out spicy and delicious.

Brother excelled most at eating—he always stood first in line to fill his bowl.

One evening inside the lodge, the smells of leather and fresh roasted meat thickened the air. After eating, everyone but Thunder gathered at the fire, working and talking about the baby's coming. Each of them had tried, without luck, to get Thunder involved in making something for her new baby. They worked quietly, trying not to stare as she paced the lodge, and they glanced her way only when her back was turned.

Without warning, Thunder swung about, glaring at everyone. "Star, you are wasting your time making that cradleboard."

Star weighed her words carefully. "Every baby should have a cradleboard, and this baby will be more important to you than any other."

"If this baby is so important," Thunder spat, "it should not have begun the way it did!"

Shrinking from Thunder's outburst, Star strained to keep her voice calm. "A mother does not always have a choice in this, and the baby certainly does not. I know the baby wants you to look past that, to see it as it truly is."

Thunder's eyes flashed with rage. "It is an enemy's spawn. I will cut its throat the moment it crawls out of me."

"Great Spirit!" Star shouted, narrowing her own eyes to slivers. "This baby's soul did not begin in the attack. It has only come to you in this way to live as your own flesh and blood!"

"It is not my flesh and blood. It is a white man's abomination!" Thunder stooped down, swiped Star's materials for the cradleboard, and flung them in the fire.

Flames crackled, shooting sparks in every direction. Singing Wind laid down the infant garment she was sewing and brushed the live coals into the fire. Maria and Victoria also put down their tiny outfits. Fear crept into Victoria's eyes. Brother, thank the Great Spirit, was already sleeping.

Singing Wind stepped away from the fire, saying she needed to fetch more firewood. Victoria released a deep breath to cover her shock, rose, and said, "Come, Maria, it is a good evening for a walk."

Star pulled up her knees and hugged them to her chest, deeply troubled by Thunder's resolve. "I fear you will regret keeping your heart closed. Please, just open yourself to your own inner spirit."

"Do not bother, Star. Words will not stop me from killing this devil."

Star shook her head. "This is your baby, Thunder. Yours, and yours alone. To destroy it would be to destroy a part of yourself." With no further word, she got up and stepped outside.

Standing in the cold, blinded by tears, Star pleaded with the Great Spirit to show Thunder her error. Eventually, Singing Wind joined her and took her by the arm. She led Star into the cooking lodge, where Victoria and Maria were rekindling the fire.

"I am sorry Thunder hurt you," Singing Wind said.

Star took a moment to compose her thoughts. "I am sure you must wonder why Thunder is so angry. I think it is important for all of you know her history with the whites and how she became pregnant. It may help you understand Thunder's hatred for the baby."

While everyone hovered over the small fire, Star alternated between Cheyenne and slow, broken Spanish. She told of the white-eyes ripping Thunder from her home, separating her from Golden Eagle before they could marry. How soldiers killed Thunder's beloved grandfather, her best friend, and her entire village. Finally, Star explained how the white trapper had brutally raped Thunder, resulting in the pregnancy.

"Before," Star said, "I could help her. Now, I cannot."

"I understand Thunder's suffering," Maria whispered, "but the sin of killing her child would be too great. The Lord would punish her severely."

"I understand too," Victoria said. "I have lost my home and family. Men have used me. But nothing would make me take the life of my child."

Protectively placing her arm around Victoria, Star continued. "We must each ask our own God to place Thunder's feet on the proper path. We can offer her love and support, but I will not support her in killing her child. Maybe her people would do such a thing, and I understand her feelings completely. But I *know* that *this* child must have a chance to live."

EIGHTEEN

Colorado, December 1879

Many miles northeast of Thunder's winter camp, Golden Eagle and his companions struggled through a patch of thorny juniper. They wanted a closer look at the Bluecoats, who were methodically destroying White Blade's Cheyenne village.

Soldiers burned tipi hides and food, taking no notice of the braves' movement among the snow-covered briars. The Apaches watched, horrified, as everything went into a great fire.

Golden Eagle thanked the spirits that they had reached the Cheyenne earlier in the day and signed to them of the danger. Through further signing, he and his friends learned that they were a Cheyenne tribe and White Blade their chief. Uniting against their common enemy, the Apaches gave White Blade's warriors the rifles taken after the ambush. The Cheyenne had only enough time to gather half of their tipis and belongings before fleeing for their lives. Meanwhile, the three Apaches had gone up the mountainside to observe the soldiers' whereabouts.

Even with more rifles, Golden Eagle thought, *the Cheyenne are hardly able to fight.* Their gaunt, sluggish warriors rode nearly starved horses. The band lacked the strength to battle against the grain-fed horses of the Bluecoats. Indeed, they barely had the strength to flee.

The Apaches watched great coils of greasy smoke rise above the mountains. After the soldiers completed the destruction of the village, they rode to their camp on the other side of the valley. Golden Eagle cursed under his breath and motioned for his friends to follow him. They moved back to the safety of some large trees at the top of a rise. A cold, damp wind whipped around them as they sat, discussing what they should do next.

"Braves might survive this cold," Crossing Wolf said gravely, "but will their children and old ones?"

"What are you trying to tell us, brother?" Golden Eagle asked.

"Even if the soldiers do not find them, many will perish without our help."

"Those are not our people, not our responsibility," Two Feathers said adamantly.

"We are all in need of help," Golden Eagle responded. "We can hunt and fight for them, and they can feed and shelter us until spring."

"It is folly to trust the Cheyenne or anything unknown," Two Feathers insisted. "What about finding Talks Like Thunder? She could be dead or with another man."

"No, my impetuous brother," Golden Eagle said, used to his

outbursts. "We will only know when we find her, and we cannot continue searching until the snow melts. In the meantime, the Cheyenne might want us to help them survive."

The Apaches did not enter the Cheyenne camp empty-handed. Each brave carried a deer carcass on horseback with him. The tribe welcomed them for the second time that day. Hungry women butchered the venison with shaking hands, and children pulled the meat from roasting sticks even before it was cooked.

Chief White Blade stood outside his lodge, pleased to see his people with plenty to eat. A fierce-faced man, the chief had won his position through his extraordinary fighting ability. He had lived as a daring warrior, and the eagle feathers in his headdress spoke of his uncommon bravery. Both sides of his chest showed divots where his skin had healed over damaged muscle after the Cheyenne Sun Dance. As part of the ritual, elders had inserted slender bones—white blades—through his flesh, then attached them to long straps draped from a pole. He had hung—suspended by his flesh—for days, until his body's weight had ripped the bones free. The disfigurement proved the old chief had no fear of pain.

White Blade had survived many trials, from which he drew his wisdom, and he had a pure heart. Despite the Cheyenne's grave poverty, he nor his people, ever refused to help those of any tribe in need. Now, in his own people's time of need, strangers had come to share their own weapons and bounty.

White Blade wanted to meet with these friendly strangers. He sent his best signer to the newcomers to invite them to share his evening meal. Once he learned their origin, he might be able to find one in his band who knew their language.

When the Apaches stepped into the warm dimness of White Blade's lodge, they found another warrior there. White Blade raised his hand in greeting, then spoke to the other man in Cheyenne. After a moment, the warrior addressed the visitors in their own language. "Chief White Blade says to tell you that I, his friend Buffalo Killer, have been among his people for several moons. I am the only one among them who can communicate his words to you."

All three Apaches greeted Buffalo Killer, then Crossing Wolf asked, "You are not of the Cheyenne?"

Buffalo Killer grinned. "I am of the Blackfoot people, who live a long way to the north. Years ago, Bluecoats defeated my hunting band and took us to a reservation far to the southeast. I made some Apache friends before I escaped."

"We have much in common," Crossing Wolf said with a smile.

After a short silence, White Blade invited the Apaches to sit and eat. During the meal, he thanked them for coming out of hiding to warn him about the soldiers. That and bringing weapons and meat to his band showed that they held to the traditional warrior ideals of the past. "The old rules are the only rules," the chief said emphatically. "Too many of the young warriors in this village think only of themselves. Such an attitude brings danger to the whole village."

As Buffalo Killer translated, Crossing Wolf saw Two Feathers shift with discomfort. No doubt he regretted his childishness in objecting to helping the Cheyenne.

After they finished eating, Crossing Wolf said to the chief, "Tell me, what are you planning for the future? Do you have some place to hide from the soldiers?"

"There is little to plan, and nowhere left to hide in this part of the country." The pain lines on White Blade's gaunt face spoke of his anguish even more clearly than his words. "When the snow melts, the soldiers will come. Only Grandmother's Land can provide us safety."

"Are you saying the soldiers cannot go to that place?" Two Feathers asked.

"Yes. It is a different land, ruled by a queen who will allow us to live there in peace." The old man took out his pipe. "Long ago," he related, "the English people fought the French and won from them the ground now called Grandmother's Land. It grieves me to leave these mountains where the bones of our ancestors rest. There is talk, though, that even some tribes have turned against us. I hear some of the Sioux are selling the Black Hills to the Wasichu, bringing shame to all tribes. While red traitors grow fat serving these strangers, we grow thin serving the Great Spirit."

"Yes, what you say is true," Crossing Wolf said. "Other Indians have told us their people surrendered just for sweet grit, black drink, and firewater."

White Blade nodded grimly. "And so it is with all tribes. We must be thankful for those who wish to live free as our fathers and grandfathers did. Many such believers have escaped the reservations and come to fight. Among us now are Arapaho, Oglala,

Lakota, Santee, and even some of our old enemies, the Blackfoot." The old man grinned at Buffalo Killer.

"I like the sound of this Grandmother's Land," Golden Eagle said. "Perhaps when we find Talks Like Thunder, we will join you there. When do you plan to go?"

"As soon as the mountain passes are open. To see you there would make this old man smile. We plan to follow the North Star, cross the Bull Mountains, and continue north to the Bear Paws. Two suns' ride beyond them is the Medicine Line—a line that can be seen only on white men's maps. It runs a very great distance from east to west, between the United States and Grandmother's Land. Sitting Bull and his Sioux people have settled at a place called Wood Mountain. Unless things change, you will find me with the Sioux near Clay Creek. If I am not there, they will know where my new camp is."

"Then you can expect us," Crossing Wolf said as his friends nodded in agreement.

"Grandmother's Land is a cold place, but buffalo are still plentiful in summer. We will be able to find plenty of meat and make warm clothing. We will have good winters, for Grandmother will not let the soldiers come and kill us."

White Blade went on to explain that his old friend Sitting Bull had gone there three winters ago. "I am sure his people are safe and content. I should have taken his advice earlier. He predicted the Wasichus would never stop until they had all our land. He was a man of vision. I was the fool."

Crossing Wolf saw the anguish in the old man's eyes. "Grandfather, do not talk of yourself like that. You are a great chief and a wise man. No one could have known the palefaces would have such black hearts."

As Buffalo Killer translated, the chief nodded sadly.

The Apaches thanked the chief for the meal and excused themselves. Golden Eagle and Two Feathers went to tend the horses, and Crossing Wolf returned to the lodge the Apaches shared with a Cheyenne family. He added dry wood to the fire, then sat and stared into the red-orange blaze. His fondness for the old chief made him feel responsible for the villagers' welfare. He decided to lead a hunt with Golden Eagle and Two Feathers the next day. He hoped to find enough game to feed the people and begin a food reserve. Since soldiers occupied the lowlands, they would hunt higher in the mountains.

The next morning, waist-high drifts in the mountains made hunting more difficult than expected. The Apaches had never seen so much snow. Their winded, overworked horses struggled to stay on their feet. Though the clouds had drifted away and the sun shone on them, the air was far below freezing. Strong wind bit through their clothing, causing their limbs and fingers to go numb.

The neighing of a horse above carried through the icy air. They dismounted, dropped to their knees, and started to crawl up the snowy incline.

"Enemies?" Crossing Wolf mouthed.

"Better to be sure," Golden Eagle signed.

At the top of the rise, two horses stood despondently, heads lowered, tails turned to the wind. A sudden sound at the Apache's backs caused them to spin around and see two Indians in Army uniforms facing them.

The fear pumping through Golden Eagle's veins caused his world to slow to a crawl. All five men fumbled for their weapons. Crossing Wolf, hands wrapped in rags, responded first. He shot a scout, then cursed when the second shell did not fire. The other scout's bullet slammed into Golden Eagle's shoulder as Two Feathers' bullet buried itself in the scout's heart.

Golden Eagle groaned as he fell, blood soaking into his shirt. He curled up in the soft snow, pressing his numbed fingers against the wound. Although it pained him, he knew it would not take his life.

Two Feathers rushed forward to help him. Crossing Wolf pulled an Army blanket from one of the scouts and wrapped it around Golden Eagle's shoulders, saying, "If the patrol discovers them missing, they will come looking."

Together, Crossing Wolf and Two Feathers carefully helped Golden Eagle on his horse. They loaded the scouts' bodies onto their Army horses and led the horses behind their own, back to camp.

When they reached the Cheyenne village, most of the people came running to see what the Apaches had brought. A cheer came from the villagers when they saw the two dead scouts. The men helped Golden Eagle dismount and handed him to a group of women who would look after his wound.

Amid the people's praise and backslapping, Crossing Wolf removed the scouts' weapons from their horses. He handed the animals over to a group of thinly clad young boys, who stripped off the scouts' clothes. *Desperate to stay warm,* he thought as he strode to the chief's lodge.

White Blade stood outside his tipi, watching the fresh snow slowly float to the ground. When Crossing Wolf arrived, a rifle under each arm, the chief opened his hands to receive one of the weapons. He looked at it closely. *Barely used, taken from soldiers or scouts. The Army will find our camp at any time.* He returned the gun to Crossing Wolf then weighed the potential Army attack against traveling through the falling snow. A gust of wind hurled snow into the air, obscuring his view of the countryside. He smiled, certain this was the beginning of a great snowstorm, one which would stop the soldiers until spring.

NINETEEN

Colorado, December 1879

Following the village women's hand signing, Golden Eagle entered the dimly lit lodge of the shaman, Little Crazy Wolf. The young Cheyenne medicine man resembled no other shaman Golden Eagle had ever seen. His blue-black hair lay in soft waves, mostly hidden under the gray-and-black wolf pelt covering his head. The pelt's empty front paws hung down either side of his elegantly painted face. A robe of glistening white ermine hung around his broad shoulders. He was quite a spectacle to behold.

Later, Golden Eagle would learn much more about Little Crazy Wolf. The shaman never carried a weapon; his strong medicine always protected him from any adversary. When not attending the infirm, he usually meditated in the forest, under his favorite medicine tree. He bore a reputation as a deep thinker—best left alone with his thoughts. Some said he obtained his name when a careless person had interrupted his contemplation. Rumor had it that he had inherited the wavy hair from his grandfather, a Spanish prince.

Upon examining Golden Eagle's wound, Little Crazy Wolf found the bullet passed through the shoulder, making surgery unnecessary. He dressed the wound and performed a healing ritual to drive out evil spirits. The constant pounding of the shaman's drum nearly drove Golden Eagle mad. The next morning, he reluctantly concluded the ritual had succeeded. That, or the special blend of herbs and aloe vera mixed with bear grease, had sealed the wound completely.

Later that morning, Crossing Wolf and Two Feathers visited Golden Eagle. They extended an invitation from White Blade for the three Apaches to visit him again. Golden Eagle accepted, and his friends helped him to the chief's lodge through the heavily falling snow, already knee-deep.

After greeting the chief and Buffalo Killer, Golden Eagle's companions helped him to sit in comfort. Through Buffalo Killer, White Blade asked about the injury. Golden Eagle assured the chief he would heal, and White Blade thanked him for risking his life for the band.

A moment later, Two Feathers asked the chief why such an honorable man had ordered his people to run, leaving half his village's possessions behind. He added quickly, before Buffalo Killer translated, that the chief was obviously not a coward.

The wise old man understood and chose to ignore the near insult. He tried to answer the young man's question truthfully, explaining his people no longer had power. "We have lost our greatest shamans," the chief said sadly. "It is a long and complicated story."

"In my village," Golden Eagle said with a smile, "Ghost Face was the season for long stories. They brought much pleasure to an idle time."

The old chief's brown eyes lit up at the curiosity of these young Apaches. He took a long draw on his pipe, then set it aside. Leaning against his willow-limbed backrest, he began to speak in a low, rhythmic voice.

"Centuries ago, the prophet Sweet Medicine came to the Cheyenne people. Before his coming, the Cheyenne were bad, living without chiefs, warriors, or any sense of kindred. They were even killing one another."

"We have heard of Sweet Medicine through Indians at the white-eyes' fort," Crossing Wolf said. "He was a prophet, no?"

"Yes, he was a great prophet," the old chief answered promptly as a smile enlivened his wrinkled face. "I will tell you the story as my people have told it for many generations."

The braves shifted into a comfortable position, anticipating a long tale.

White Blade told them of the birth of Sweet Medicine and the miracles he performed at an early age. Most notably, he killed a small buffalo calf that provided an abundant supply of meat for hundreds of people.

"Later in life," Chief White Blade continued, "Sweet Medicine disappeared from the Black Hills for four years. When he returned, he said he had been on Knaves, a sacred mountain where he had obtained special knowledge for the Cheyenne. The ancient ones had given Sweet Medicine the Sacred Arrows to take to his people. The Arrows, powerful and holy, would keep them healthy and strong. They would also reform the people's way of life and make them a great nation.

"Sweet Medicine taught the Cheyenne how to set up a proper governing system. The government would consist of forty-four chiefs. He helped the people create four military societies: the Swift Foxes, the Elks, the Bowstrings, and the Red Shields. He also instituted the custom of marriage. He taught the people that a man and woman united in ceremony must honor and respect each other.

"Four years after his return, Sweet Medicine led the Cheyenne to a campsite near Bear's Lodge Butte. The whites call it the "Devils Tower," but it is a sacred place to us. Soon after they arrived, a vision told Sweet Medicine his time on earth would soon end. Just before his death, he summoned his people together for the last time. He cautioned them about strange men who would come and take over their hunting grounds. The buffalo, he said, would disappear and be replaced by the invaders' cattle. The invaders would also bring a new animal that would help the Cheyenne in hunting."

White Blade's words stunned Golden Eagle. He remembered the old Chiricahua warriors telling him of the days before the coming of the horses. Back then, his people had used dogs to pull their pole drag sleds and move heavy loads. Then had come the first sighting of the white-eyes and their cattle beasts—both considered very odd creatures. Much sadness and loss had happened since that time. He saw the old chief's somber expression and knew his mind now wandered to some other time and place.

"In recent years," White Blade went on, "the renowned Cheyenne shaman Raven's Wing declared that a young girl would succeed him. This girl, Falling Star, displayed a strong bond with animals and great healing powers. Raven's Wing predicted Falling Star would lead the Cheyenne beyond the prophecy of Sweet Medicine. Falling Star embodied his hope for a future when the Cheyenne would rise up and reclaim their lost greatness.

"I thought perhaps I could meet Falling Star someday and ask for her guidance in these difficult times. However, a Cheyenne warrior from Falling Star's band came to my camp several moons ago. He told of an attack by Bluecoats, which he alone survived. Before the battle, Raven's Wing approached the Bluecoats to parley, and they shot him dead. During the ensuing fight, the warrior was separated from the others. When he returned shortly after the battle, he found no survivors."

"You are leading the Cheyenne's bravest warriors," Crossing Wolf declared. "Can they not save your people?"

"Cheyenne men have always been known for their bravery." White Blade paused, taking a deep, poignant breath. "But without a new vision," he murmured through taut lips, "we have no will to fight."

TWENTY

Colorado, March 1880

The pit fire and grease-soaked torches provided the only light in the lodge that night. Thunder bit down hard on the clump of rawhide to keep from screaming in agony. The excruciating pains in her womb made her thrash about like a fighting mountain lion.

Star fixed her gaze at Singing Wind and Maria. "With Thunder rolling around like this, we cannot help her. You have to hold her down." As Thunder moaned, the two girls grabbed her arms.

"Kettle's boiling!" Brother yelled as he threw another log on the fire.

Victoria took the pot of phlox, which steamed forth a wonderful smell of maple, and brought it to Star.

"Do not fight it so much, Thunder," Star pleaded as she massaged Thunder's abdomen. "Put all your strength into pushing out the baby."

Thunder barely heard, her mind consumed with pain. Yet nature continued on its course, and the rhythm of contractions went on, unaffected by her rebellion.

"The little one has nearly arrived," Star said, "but the passageway is too small. Victoria, give me the knife."

Heated in the fire earlier, the clean, sharp blade cut the obstructing flesh. Star cleaned the area with the solution of phlox to insure rapid healing.

Thunder's pain flared into unbearable agony for one final moment. Then it vanished, and in that moment of sublime relief, she heard a baby's cry.

"A boy!" Star cried with delight. She washed the vigorous newborn with warm water of dissolved feather plume and wrapped him in a soft blanket.

Maria and Singing Wind wiped the blood from Thunder's legs. "Are you all right?" Maria asked as she dabbed the perspiration from the new mother's face.

Completely spent, Thunder only nodded as she lay as limp as a willow branch.

"You have a son," Singing Wind said, kneeling and rubbing Thunder's arms. "A beautiful baby boy!"

Using a long black flint, Star severed the umbilical cord before tying it with a yucca-leaf string. As they gathered around the new arrival, Brother asked, "Can I hold him?"

Star smiled. "Maybe his mother should hold him first." Brother nodded, and they circled around Thunder. Without a word or hesitation, Star placed the small one at Thunder's bosom.

Cradling the baby in her arms, Thunder looked down and saw the distinctive nose of her grandfather. Taken aback, she closed her eyes and felt a tranquil, in-control presence in the newborn. She willed her spirit to go deeper and hear her baby's message.

"Little boy," she whispered to her son. "Little boy." As she bent her head to smell him, she detected a familiar aroma. In wonderment, she slowly drew back and stared deep into the infant's dark eyes.

"Who are you?" she asked the boy. Deeper into the spirit of the infant she moved. For several moments, mother and newborn gazed at each other. Then she knew the identity of this spirit and smiled. Within this tiny newborn baby resided her grandfather. He had returned.

"Yes, I understand." She nodded and touched his nose. "I am happy to see you again. Welcome back...*Young Fox*."

TWENTY-ONE

Colorado, April 1880

Four moons after the arrival of Golden Eagle and his friends among White Blade's people, soldiers had still not attacked. As White Blade had surmised, the mountains were assailed by an unmerciful blizzard. The wind howled for days, and dark, billowing clouds dropped snow until it piled chest high. When the storm cleared, all tracks had vanished. Such deep snow left the Army unable to move on foot or horseback.

As the snow melted, Golden Eagle grew impatient to search for Thunder once more. Thinking of her traveling alone in this dangerous land, he *had* to find her soon.

During the winter, Two Feathers had fallen in love with a Cheyenne girl. Crossing Wolf, after moons of planning the northward journey with White Blade, felt obligated to help him see it through. Golden Eagle did not blame his friends for choosing to follow the Cheyenne. He prayed to the spirits that they would find prosperity in their new lives.

One morning, White Blade ordered the tribe to prepare to start for Grandmother's Land at dawn the next day. The time had come for Golden Eagle to leave White Blade's band and find Thunder. He sought out Buffalo Killer and explained that he planned to depart the village before noon. He asked the Blackfoot to pass on his request to meet with the chief once again. Buffalo Killer soon returned with White Blade's invitation for all three Apaches to visit him.

Later, at the chief's lodge, the five men sat around the fire for the last time. Aware of the significance of the moment, White Blade took the last few stems of sweetgrass from his pouch and sprinkled them onto the hot coals. Small puffs of flame rose and fell as the fragrant aroma permeated the lodge. Golden Eagle filled his lungs with the tart, cleansing smoke. "My brothers," he said glumly, "I find it very difficult to leave you."

"You have lived among us with an empty heart," White Blade replied through Buffalo Killer.

"I must go. Yet I have deep gratitude for your people's shelter and food."

"We survived the winter by helping one another, my friend."

Crossing Wolf and Two Feathers wished Golden Eagle good fortune in finding Thunder, and White Blade blessed him for safe travel.

After translating, Buffalo Killer added, "Many of my tribe have lived in Grandmother's Land and hunted far to the south for generations. You should stay on the east side of the mountain range while you travel north; that will help you hide from the whites. As you draw near Grandmother's Land, three great buttes can be seen to the northeast from two-suns' ride away. The Medicine Line lies at the northern base of the westernmost butte. When you reach Grandmother's Land, ride east for about fifteen suns. Sitting Bull's camp is there, about a sun's ride north of the line."

Golden Eagle thanked Buffalo Killer for imparting his knowledge. After embracing everyone, he said, "We will meet soon in Grandmother's Land." As he left the tipi, a sudden sadness overcame him. He pushed it from his mind by assuring himself they would all find safety before autumn.

He departed from the village, taking only what he could carry easily: his rifle, blanket, skin of water, and a supply pack containing a few dozen bullets. Earlier, he had asked Crossing Wolf and Two Feathers to care for his mare before he bade her goodbye. The horse would have found little to eat in the mountains, and in this rugged terrain, Golden Eagle could travel as quickly on foot. He politely refused the people's offers for provisions, knowing the tribe needed food more than he did.

Warm days melted the snow quickly, putting the settlers, soldiers, and natives into motion. Word of a safe haven would spread quickly among the natives, so Thunder would probably also head to Grandmother's Land. Golden Eagle traveled west, reasoning that Thunder could not have camped unnoticed through the winter anywhere to the east.

On his fifth sun of travel, clouds gathered steadily as he walked along the base of a mountain. The slope blocked his view of the path ahead. Curious, Golden Eagle hurried around the slope until he looked upon the grandest mountain he had ever seen. The steep granite cliffs threatened to block his way, but his desire to find Thunder pressed him to take the treacherous route.

Throughout the day, as dark clouds sailed above, Golden Eagle became entangled in a series of dead ends. He reached impassable stone massifs, backtracked, scuttled over rock ledges, ascended a thousand steps, dropped five hundred, then climbed two thousand more. What he had considered a half-day's hike took more than a full day.

By sundown, repeated flashes of lightning and raw gusts of wind warned him of a building storm. With no shelter in sight, he looked only for a flat place to lie down. After much searching under a rapidly darkening sky, he found a level spot. He had no wood to make a fire and nothing to eat, so he could only hope for rest.

From under his blanket, he heard the tap of raindrops, then a battering. The downpour soon soaked through his blanket and clothes. He spent the night shivering miserably.

At dawn, he wrung out his blanket, flung it over his shoulder, and resumed his journey. The sunny morning travel made up for the previous difficult day. Despite his sticky, wet clothes and the beginning of a rumbling cough, he was in good spirits. He walked over the stone with care and found places to look ahead for a sure route.

At mid-morning he encountered a sheer cliff that provided no way to climb above or pass below. He studied the cliff for a long time, mapping in his mind the best way to cross. First, he would wait for the sun to dry the rock completely. After collecting dead shrub branches, he used some to make a fire and stacked the rest in a semicircle around the blaze. He took off his clothes and set them on the branches, then hung the remaining wet belongings beside the clothes. His Springfield, however, needed the most care. He brushed residue off a flat stone near the fire, then sat cross-legged with the rifle. He carefully twisted out the screws with his hunting knife and disassembled all that he could. After taking his damp shirt from near the fire, he used it to carefully dab water from the parts while leaving the lubricating oil. He placed the pieces in a line, close to the fire. The long time spent near the fire restored his strength. When everything had dried, he donned his clothes, reassembled the rifle, and repacked his belongings to stay securely behind him for crossing the rock face. His moccasins also went into his pack; he could not afford the least bit of slippage.

As the sun arced to its zenith, Golden Eagle slowly inched his way along the side of the cliff. Looking ahead and back, he realized —with great joy—that he had almost crossed its entire length. Clinging to the rock like a desert lizard, he pressed his toes down on a nub of stone. He released his left hand from a crack below to dig his right hand deeper into a fissure above. He wheezed in another breath as he searched for a place to plant his next step. Suddenly the toehold gave way, with only his one-handed grip keeping him aloft.

Frantically, he groped with his feet and free hand for a hold to keep him from tumbling to his death. His toes scraped against the vertical slab of rock, loosening pebbles that tapped their long way down. "All-Father," he cried, "help me find a way to safety!"

He put his left hand in the same fissure and forcefully dug both hands in as deeply as possible. Desperately looking for another foothold, he spotted a sharp rock jutting out to his right, beyond his reach. His fingers and forearms throbbed in pain, and he knew he had to find support soon. He pulled himself up until he faced his hands, then bent his knees and arched his back. Thus, he shifted his weight to his forearms against the cliff, further straining his nearly spent fingers. He swung from side to side, gaining momentum, until he snagged the jagged rock with his outstretched foot. Resting diagonally, he took in several huge draughts of air.

Regaining his breath, he saw a crack in the stone above, just big enough to push his fingers into. Despite his aching, bleeding foot, he worked his way to a plateau where he would be able to resume his journey. He sat and tended the cut. After washing the wound with water from his waterskin, he found the gash in the ball of his foot went bone deep. He sliced off part of his deerskin jacket, bound the wound tightly, and gave thanks to All-Father. Once healed, the scar would always remind him of his answered prayer. He downed the remainder of his water to wash away the phlegm in his throat, then pulled on his moccasins.

Careful of his wounded foot, he hobbled down the now-gentle slope for the rest of the day. The sun hung low to the west when a stream came within sight. Tracks on the bank caused him to yelp hoarsely in great surprise, "Fresh horse prints!"

They were unshod horses, not from Bluecoats, and no one had bothered to conceal them. He remembered the last time he had found an uncovered trail like this. *Thunder?*

He filled his waterskin and followed the tracks.

Rambling along the creek, he watched a bronze shaft of sunlight spread itself across the sparkling water. Golden Eagle's stride was sluggish. Away from the sun's brightness, he looked haggard; his lean, sharply-angled jaw made him appear much older than his years. A knife was tucked into a wide piece of dirty yellow gingham wrapped around his waist, and a carbine hung from his shoulder. His once well-crafted leggings were badly frayed and held together with strips of knotted rawhide.

When the light grew too dim to trace the trail, he looked for a place to camp. After shivering through the previous night and the day of walking, his cough had worsened, and exhaustion seeped into every muscle and bone. Slim rations all winter had weakened his body, and the penetrating chill had caused his illness to advance unopposed. He hobbled up the hillside and decided to camp among a grove of towering evergreens.

Shedding his belongings, he caught a faint whiff of smoke. As much as he wanted to rest, he could not without knowing if those who had made the fire were friends or enemies. Overcoming his fatigue, he limped along in the dim twilight until he came upon a camp. He counted five horses and saw the outlines of four people around the campfire. *Maybe another lurks nearby.* Listening closely, he heard the voices of women. Fear abated, he stifled a cough and soundlessly moved to a closer tree.

He could not discern faces, but one figure held an infant. *A child without warriors' protection? Odd. Could Thunder be among them?* So often he had fantasized finding her, and many other times he had imagined her just at hand, each time more disappointing than the last. *I dare not raise my hopes too high, I may be wrong again.*

A flame leaped up, and to his astonishment, it revealed a white boy in a settler's shirt.

Standing rock-still, Golden Eagle looked through the split of two branches. In addition to the boy, he saw three young women in native dress, one nursing a baby. From an occasional word he recognized, the women seemed to be speaking in Cheyenne. One voice had the distinct sound of Thunder's, but how could she know Cheyenne? If he heard her voice just once more, he would know for sure.

Suddenly, a cough burst out of him. So engrossed in his guesswork, he had not even felt it coming.

He heard the boy yell something in English, pointing in his direction. Two from the group grabbed their weapons. The youth drew his hunting knife, yelling, and raced toward him, brandishing it menacingly.

Golden Eagle held up his Springfield, pointed to the sky, his finger on the trigger. He stepped from behind the tree. "*Ya-ta-hey*, Golden Eagle, Apache!" he shouted, ready to bolt.

"Golden Eagle!" pierced the air as the woman with the baby at her breast sprang to her feet. She yelled to the boy, who stopped and lowered his weapon, then she gave the infant to another woman.

"Thunder!" he cried, knowing beyond all doubt that he had found her. He dropped his rifle in bewilderment. *She has a child... she has married someone else...* His mind raced. *That youth in settler's clothes? No, he is only a boy...perhaps she is just holding another's baby.* His hope soared once again. She had waited for him, just as she promised. Then hope fell as quickly as it had risen: when she jumped up, she had been nursing. *That baby has to be hers. She didn't wait for me...she belongs to another. Maybe I should just leave. But if I do, I will always wonder why she had broken her promise.*

Thunder ran toward Golden Eagle, and he to her. She leaped into his open arms, squeezed him tightly, and pressed her cheek against his as unexpected tears brimmed her eyes and overflowed. She felt the medallion, made for him so many moons ago, enveloped between them. He had remained chaste for her, but her baby proved that she had no right to say the same. Would he understand? She would have to explain soon, but not now. For the first time in her life, she could not think of anything to say.

Her strong, desperate embrace should have reassured him, but Golden Eagle still wondered. Yet she held him tightly for so long that she must have a reason. He circled his arms snugly around her, sweeping her into a close embrace of his own. For an endless moment they stayed that way, until Thunder placed her hand on the back of his neck. "You have a fever."

"I was chilled by rain last night," Golden Eagle rasped. Releasing her, he said softly, "I saw you nursing a baby. It pains me to think you have married someone else."

She shook her head, whispering only one word: "Rape."

Golden Eagle's body went limp, and his heart sank like a heavy stone. Some man had molested Thunder, just as Crossing Wolf and Two Feathers had surmised. A storm of fury welled within him, and he yearned to know the man's name. *That man should die at my hand a thousand times to atone for his wicked deed.* Then guilt overcame him for having failed to find her in time to protect her.

Thunder broke the grim silence. "He is dead. It is a long story for a later time." She clasped his hand and led him to camp. The baby started crying, so Thunder carried him away, telling Golden Eagle, "Step over to the fire, and I will join you soon. My Cheyenne friend is a great shaman. She will restore your health."

TWENTY-TWO

Colorado, April 1880

By the fire, Star prepared an herbal drink that would relieve Golden Eagle's fever. If he did not overwork himself during the next few suns, he should recover quickly.

She pointed to the rough deerskin wrapping on his foot. "What is this?"

"I cut it while crossing a cliff."

"It needs to be redressed. Lie down so I can raise your foot easily." After he did so, she removed the bandage, cleaned the wound, and began to wrap a clean strip of cloth around his foot.

"Where are you traveling?" Golden Eagle asked. "Grandmother's Land?"

"So, you know about it too," Star said. "Yes, we are—after we find the Cheyenne. I must bring my medicine bundle to them. I believe its power will help them begin a new way of life."

"I spent the winter with White Blade's Cheyenne band. He told the story of Sweet Medicine, but nothing of such a bundle."

Amazed, Star dropped the bandage. "You have seen my people!"

"Yes. They are also going northward to Grandmother's Land. How will your medicine bundle help them?"

"I follow the steps of Raven's Wing—"

"Are you Falling Star?" Golden Eagle exclaimed, staring wide-eyed.

Puzzled, Star said, "Yes."

He immediately sat up. "White Blade thought you had been killed in battle!"

"I was wounded and near death when Thunder found me." Star picked up the bandage and resumed dressing his foot. "She nursed me back to health."

"White Blade will be very glad to see you alive and would welcome any help you can offer."

"Let us go find them!" she cried.

Golden Eagle smiled and informed her of the hazard of searching for the Cheyenne with so many soldiers near them. "I have already planned to meet White Blade at Sitting Bull's encampment. It is safer to go directly to Grandmother's Land."

"Yes, that is best."

Later, Singing Wind volunteered to care for Young Fox, and she, Star, and Brother retired for the night. Golden Eagle and Thunder sat together at the campfire. Golden Eagle first asked her what had happened to her ear, and she related the story and her hatred for

Polecat. After a long silence, Golden Eagle gently asked her to tell him about the rape.

Thunder drew a deep breath. *Does he understand what he is asking of me?* She mentally winced at the thought of reliving that day. *But he knows nothing and deserves to know what happened.*

"As I struck a weasel in my snare," she began, "a trapper hit me from behind."

Golden Eagle nodded. "How did that happen?"

The implication stung Thunder. "He hid behind a tree," she bellowed, "two steps away from the snare, waiting for me to deal with the animal! I know you would expect more of me as an apprentice warrior—"

"Thunder!" Golden Eagle cut in, then lowered his voice. "I am not accusing you of carelessness. After your grandfather gave me warrior status, I learned much from Crossing Wolf, especially about tracking. We should always be willing to learn to become better warriors. When we are defeated but survive, the spirits have blessed us with a chance to learn from that defeat. So we learn, and we will not be defeated in that way again."

Thunder released a pent-up breath and silently thanked the spirits for Golden Eagle's understanding. He saw her as blameless, as she had learned to see herself, but he had done so quickly and independently. In this way, he dispelled the last of her shame.

After they had crawled under their blankets, Thunder drifted off to sleep knowing she loved the right man.

The next morning, Thunder asked Brother to surrender his horse so Golden Eagle could ride on a saddle. Brother reluctantly agreed and mounted between the supplies on the packhorse.

That night, while Star looked after Young Fox, Golden Eagle and Thunder again stayed by the campfire. He asked her how she had spent the past two years. Her long story began with her time at the school and concluded with their recent departure from the winter camp. "Throughout the winter, Victoria had much difficulty breathing, and Maria knew she had to take her mother home. We gave them rifles, pistols, ammunition, along with medicines from Star, and many hides from Singing Wind. Everyone cried as we hugged one another and said goodbye."

Golden Eagle pondered Thunder's story. "So, you journeyed across the entire land of the Mescaleros and beyond! No wonder we could not track you down." He bore his eyes into hers. "Thunder, were you running away from me?"

"I have never thought of it that way," she said, then paused. "Perhaps you are right."

Golden Eagle imagined the guilt she must have felt. "I can see why you did that."

She looked solemnly at him, and he felt her gratitude and relief. "I let the soldiers separate us," he continued. "I wish with all my heart that I could have defended you."

"Do not blame yourself," Thunder said. "The spirits took us on different paths. Now they have brought us together, and we can thank them for that."

"Yes, but your path has burdened you with a white man's child."

After a moment, Thunder said softly. "Most of our people would have killed the baby. During my pregnancy, I would have done the same. But once I gave birth to him, I knew I could not kill him. I love him, and I will fight to the death anyone who means him harm."

Collecting himself, he said, "Of course, I understand. He is your child." Golden Eagle stood. "It is late, and time to rest."

After they walked silently to the bedrolls, Golden Eagle kissed Thunder on the forehead. He lay down, pulled his blanket around himself, and let his mind drift. *I have never known a man to love a woman who had a white-eyes' baby. Would the spirits disapprove of me raising the child of a white man?*

He thought back to childhood, recalling as much as he could of what his father had told him about life and the spirit world. He rolled over, wishing he could somehow ask his father for advice. Slowly, he realized there were no teachings to guide him. Not until the waning moon had begun its descent, he finally allowed himself to sleep.

The next morning, Golden Eagle saw Thunder seated on a log, nursing the infant. "What is the name of the boy?" he asked.

"Young Fox," Thunder proudly replied. "When I saw him for the first time, I knew he was Grandfather returned to this world."

Golden Eagle turned his head and looked sidelong at Thunder. "Your grandfather has chosen to live another life among us?"

Thunder smiled, lifted Young Fox from her breast, and held him up to Golden Eagle. "He is a fine boy, you will see. Just hold him for a moment."

Golden Eagle took the baby in his arms and beheld his facial features and eyes. *Thunder is right. He could be no other than the spirit of Gray Fox.* He heard a slight cry, then saw a hint of a smile. When Young Fox's hand squeezed Golden Eagle's index finger, any doubts about becoming this boy's father were dispelled. *I now have a chance to repay my debt to one of those who shaped me into a man.*

Realizing how misplaced his thoughts had been, Golden Eagle laughed. To have the chance to nurture the *nantan* who had cared for him would be a great privilege. He looked into Thunder's eyes.

MARJORIE CARTER & RANDAL NERHUS

"I love you, Thunder. And Young Fox. I will be honored to spend my life with you."

Thunder looked at him with pure delight.

"Your grandfather has returned to us," he continued. "To know that brings me such happiness that I cannot imagine my life without the two of you."

Thunder gave him the most beautiful smile he had ever seen. "Our lives together will be joyful." She held out Grinning Bear's bone-handled hunting knife. "After the massacre, I needed a weapon. I only had the pendant from my grandfather, so I gave it to your father's soul in return for his knife. But it belongs with you."

Golden Eagle thought back in wonder. "Was the pendant a sandstone thunderbird?"

"How could you know that?"

"I found it while Crossing Wolf, Two Feathers, and I prepared our people's remains for cremation."

Thunder pondered for a moment. "I felt so guilty leaving them behind, but I had no choice. It never crossed my mind someone would care for them. To know you did that has taken a great burden from me."

"And I am very pleased your gift rests with my father's soul." Golden Eagle looked at her and smiled. "Keep the knife for now. I am sure you will put it to good use."

After their morning meal, Thunder told everyone, "Since Golden Eagle knows the way to Grandmother's Land, he will lead us."

They had no choice but to keep moving northward. Camping anywhere for more than one night would increase the chance of discovery.

That night, after putting Young Fox down to sleep, Thunder and Golden Eagle again sat alone by the campfire. Golden Eagle looked her in the eyes, and said, "When we talked two nights ago..."

Thunder immediately felt her spine stiffen. *I thought we had already settled everything. Why is he bringing it up again?*

"You called yourself an apprentice warrior."

Disturbed by the reminder, Thunder said sharply, "Yes, I said that."

Remaining calm, Golden Eagle reached into his pouch and pulled out a flint arrowhead. "You lost this some time ago, and I thought my wife and fellow warrior might need it."

Thunder took the arrowhead in her hand and looked at it in the firelight. Although her eyes were focused on the arrowhead, her thoughts were somewhere else entirely. *He called me his wife...*

"Where did you find it?" she finally asked, her voice quivering.

"Oh," Golden Eagle, said smiling, "I may tell you someday."

Thunder smiled too, remembering the hole she saw in her arrow pouch after the ambush. "You are right, my husband, it is mine. Thank you for returning it to me."

Golden Eagle rose and kissed her, then swept her up in his embrace. He picked up the blanket they had been sitting on, and they left the camp hand in hand.

"Promise me one thing," Thunder said firmly.

"Yes, what is it?"

Thunder felt Golden Eagle grip her hand tighter, and a smile crept to her lips. "Find a place without ants."

The Moon of the New Grass came and went as they meandered northward through the mountains. Always alert to any movement, the band skirted around all signs of white people.

Everyone kept vigil, continually looking for new places of cover, after leaving the other shelter behind. Their food supply exhausted, they gathered whatever they could find at the end of each day.

Brother set himself apart from the band, as he had when setting up winter camp. He worked only minimally and further burdened the others. Yet, they tolerated it, allowing him to adjust to their life on the move.

Late one afternoon, the sun far to the west, the band found a safe place to make camp. In the waning light, they managed to find only a few wild onions and tubers. Singing Wind cleaned the plants, threw them into boiling water, and served everyone a bowl of watery soup.

As Brother sat staring at his half-empty bowl, his thoughts wandered into memory...

After a hard day's work, when he had just finished chores with Joey and his dad, his mother yelled, "Suppertime!" He was so hungry, he could hardly wait for the table prayer to finish. Then, finally, he wolfed down fresh bread, meat, and potatoes, all with warm milk.

Brother took a spoonful of soup, and it made him sick. He flung his bowl to the ground. "I hate eating this disgusting soup every day!"

Young Fox awoke and began to cry. Thunder glared at him fiercely. "Shut up, Brother!"

Brother stood and shouted. "All we do is ride, sleep, and eat slop!"

"We have to, Brother," Singing Wind said gently, "or we will die."

"I want to be with my people, not you!" Brother declared.

Golden Eagle rose and looked down at Brother. "We will take you back to your people as soon as we can."

Brother looked around, stung by the words and what they meant. *What will happen to me?* He lowered his head and began to cry. He didn't know what he wanted. Other white people, strangers, might hurt him. He felt helpless and alone.

"You need to know the skills of survival," Golden Eagle said, stooping over and pulling out some snares from the packs. "You have refused to learn until now. I will teach you if you wish." He held out a snare.

It dawned on Brother that he had given the others very little help. Ashamed of himself, he accepted the snare and looked at Golden Eagle. "Yes, I want to learn."

Golden Eagle smiled. "Let us find a good place to set it. You might have meat in the morning."

Brother nodded. If he helped the others by providing meat, they'd value and praise him, and he'd deserve it. Maybe someday, if Golden Eagle helped him, he could be strong and smart too. He could become a warrior! He rose and strode into the woods alongside Golden Eagle, absorbing his every word.

Wyoming Territory, May 1880

One night, as the others slept, Star lay wondering. How could she and her bundle lead the Cheyenne to a new way of life while separated from them? Maybe she should go alone and look for White Blade's band, even though it would be dangerous. Anxious for instruction, she slept intermittently until she freed her spirit to travel wherever it chose, and a vision came to her:

At the bank of the river, beneath the wall of stone, the great deer passed her. She followed the buck into a stone maze, but he quickly vanished into its intricate pathways. She sprinted around, desperately searching for him, until she was exhausted and could only stand catching her breath.

Star awoke, the vision fresh and vivid in her mind. After all this time, to see the deer and the ornate stone wall again! Yet after she pondered the vision for a while, it still did not make sense.

Suddenly, the face of her teacher, Raven's Wing, appeared to her. The old man seemed to speak to her, delivering a message into her thoughts. *The spirits have much to tell you,* he informed her. *Find the right place to summon them.*

After many suns of traveling in the forested mountains, the band emerged into a small valley divided by a meandering stream. They made camp on the stream's bank.

The next morning, Singing Wind saddled her mare and rode up a mountain and into the calm forest. With her bow in hand, she resolved to bring home an abundance of fresh meat for the coming days.

She searched the mountains for much of the day but saw no signs of big game. Disheartened, she looked through the trees down to the valley floor and decided to try her luck there. The Great Spirit must have ridden with her, for when she reached the vale, a large elk sprang before her. As the arrow pierced his heart,

Singing Wind thanked the elk for giving his life to save hers. She chanted an old hunter's prayer:

> I am a warrior like you.
> We must give our lives
> That others may carry on.
> So have no regrets my friend,
> We will meet again
> In the place where
> There is no pain or death.

If honored correctly, Singing Wind believed, the animal's spirit would return to earth twice. She prayed that both of his new lives would last longer than this one.

Her ritual complete, she made a sled to take the elk home. She was near the camp when Brother turned and saw the bounty. He fell to his knees and raised his arms, yelling, "Thank you, Lord!"

Everyone laughed, feeling the same.

That evening, the group ate roasted elk with gusto and belched loudly to compliment Singing Wind's cooking. As they licked the last of the grease from their fingers, Golden Eagle reflected on what he had seen that day. The abundant grass would restore the horses' strength if they had a few suns to graze. The trees and brush lining the mountainside would provide ideal cover for escape if necessary. He felt content and sure of the small group's safety.

"We will stay here for a few sleeps and wait for the meat and hide to cure," he told the others.

"I've never shot a gun," Brother said. "Will you teach me?"

Golden Eagle thought for a moment, then said to everyone, "We have two pistols and two rifles, with about twenty bullets for each. Thunder will only protect Young Fox, not fight. Since Singing Wind is the best shot with a pistol, she and Brother will carry those. Star and I will carry the rifles." Golden Eagle turned his eyes back to Brother. "I will instruct you how to shoot tomorrow morning."

"I need to leave at dawn and journey alone for a few sleeps," Star said, "to petition the spirits."

"We wish you well," Golden Eagle acceded, "and wait for your return."

The next morning, Golden Eagle trained Brother in the use of the pistol. He demonstrated how it worked, how to care for it, how to take it apart, and how to load it. Finally, he told Brother to shoot at the knot in the center of a tall stump to test his aim. Brother held up the pistol with one hand and began to squeeze the trigger.

"Wait!" Golden Eagle ordered. "The gun will kick back and hurt your wrist."

Brother looked at him with a puzzled stare. "My dad shot a pistol one-handed."

"Yes, but you are not that strong. Also, using two hands will keep your aim steady."

Brother brought up the pistol with both hands and quickly fired. The gun kicked back so hard that he almost lost hold of it. "Ouch! This pistol really has power." The bullet hit the ground a few paces short of the stump.

Ignoring Brother's remark, Golden Eagle took the gun and placed another bullet in the chamber. "Try again but listen carefully."

Brother took the gun and pointed it at the stump.

"Hold the gun as steady as you can and line up your sights on the knot. Now take a deep breath and hold it. Keep your sights in line with the knot as you squeeze the trigger slowly."

Brother fired and nicked the upper edge of the stump.

"You need much more practice," Golden Eagle said, "but we have too few shells to use for that." He ended the lesson and led Brother back to camp. *No matter how well he can shoot, we barely have enough ammunition for one skirmish at most. With only two rifles, we stand little chance of surviving a gunfight.*

Amidst a strong breeze and just before sunset, Star came upon a creek and made camp. She sensed the spirits were near, lifting her mood.

After building a fire on the creek's sandy bank, she walked out five paces and marked a circle around it. In this sacred space, she danced and sang chants to invoke the spirits. Before long, her eyes began to narrow then glaze as she released her spirit to ride the wind. She crumpled to the ground and a vision consumed her.

The deer darted into the stone maze, escaping Star's view. Her frantic search to find the deer left her breathless. The hillock of stone that she faced sparked her curiosity, and she studied it carefully. At the level of her heart was a round opening, just wider than the spread of her hand. Peering into the dark tunnel she saw, deep inside, a small cedar log, weathered and cracked as if by scores of years resting there.

The intense smell of soil brought Star back to consciousness. She lay prone in a straight line, her face pressed against Mother Earth. Her arms extended beyond her head, the palms of her hands resting flat against the soil. *The spirits have brought me back to the present.* She forced her fingers to move. Slowly, she brought life back into her limbs, drew her hands alongside her torso, and shifted her weight to them. Sliding her legs underneath her, she brought herself to a cross-legged position.

The fire had burned down to embers, and she gazed into the glowing coals. The vision, Star concluded, had shown her the place where the spirits wished her to leave the medicine bundle. *The spirits do not want me to deliver it to the Cheyenne. They intend it to serve the Cheyenne of a later time...My bundle will not help my people for many generations...* Tears came to her eyes. *As Sweet Medicine foretold, they would suffer much from the whites and struggle to keep their ways. Still, they would survive, and hope would live on with them. One day in the future they would rise again.* With that in mind, she lay down and slept.

In a dream, Star stood in the stone maze. She saw the cedar log through the eyes of another person, living in a future time. But something was very different, very wrong. Mother Earth herself, Star suddenly realized, languished in pain and fatigue. The whites dominated in this future time and savagely mistreated the earth.

Star's deer totem appeared at her side. *In the generations to come, the line of spoken tradition preserved by the Cheyenne shamans will be fragmented. The future will bring chaos, a lawless decadence, much like before the coming of Sweet Medicine. A shaman will come to wake the Cheyenne, and they, in turn, will wake all people. This shaman will need the secret knowledge of the ancients, and your bundle will preserve that knowledge. Prepare your bundle to endure until that time.*

Star jolted awake to find that morning had arrived. People in the distant future of her vision, she realized, would consider her bundle strange and unfamiliar. She would need to help them understand it.

She rose and scrounged the area for hardwoods unlikely to decompose over the long wait in hiding. She finally found a fallen hickory branch, long with many offshoots, yet straight and thick enough for her purpose. She could not cut the extremely hard, dry wood with her knife, so she dragged the branch to her makeshift camp.

After starting a small fire, she placed firewood nearly upright to create a high, narrow flame. As the blaze grew in strength, she found a flat stone and placed it near the fire. She positioned the branch in the flame, burned one end off, then rubbed it smooth on the stone. Likewise, she burned and smoothed the other end. Having completed one stick, she positioned the branch to burn off the next. By noon, she had completed four sticks as long as her forearm, all the width of a lance.

She sighed deeply and placed her knife in the fire. While the blade heated, she peeled the bark off the sticks. Resting one stick on her crossed legs, she used her hot knife to burn designs lengthwise into the smooth surface. Choosing her symbols carefully, she told the story of the creation of the universe and of life. Illustrating the history of the Cheyenne on the second and third sticks came simply and quickly for her. The final stick, however, proved much more difficult. She searched deep within her spirit to bring forth the correct symbols. Finally, she burned a series of representations that a future shaman could decipher. That shaman would then have the knowledge to teach the Cheyenne to once again know themselves and the world. She finished at sunset and fell into a deep sleep.

When Star awoke the following morning, she gathered up her

bundle and the design-covered sticks and started back to camp. Early in the afternoon, she noticed a charred cedar tree, split from a lightning strike. Looking around, she saw many fragments of the tree lying near the trunk. Spying a burnt branch of the same width as the small log in her vision, she picked it up and gave thanks to the Great Spirit. Soon afterward, she reached the campsite to find Singing Wind caring for Young Fox and the others bathing in the stream.

After exchanging greetings, Singing Wind pointed to the branch. "What is that for?"

"I need to make a strong shelter for my bundle." Seeing the axe resting on a pile of firewood, Star headed toward it.

"Why does your bundle need a shelter?" Singing Wind asked as she laid Young Fox in his cradleboard.

"My vision tells me to return it to Mother Earth," Star said, retrieving the axe. She cropped one end of the branch smooth. Then she chopped through the branch, producing a stub as long as the width of her hand. She tossed the stub to Singing Wind. "Here, whittle the edge of this into a cap for me."

Singing Wind pulled out her knife. "Is not your bundle for your people?"

"Yes," Star said as she cut the log to the length of her arm. "But the bundle is not safe with anyone now, for I have seen that it will lie hidden for generations. My duty lies in placing it where the spirits wish."

When Star finished chopping, she saw Singing Wind had stopped whittling, and now looked far into the distance. Star knew that her friend, abducted and stripped of her family and people, lacked a sense of meaning in her life. "Singing Wind, I know it will be very difficult for me to find the place for my bundle. With

Golden Eagle and Thunder responsible for Young Fox and Brother, I can only rely on you. Will you help me?"

Singing Wind turned her gaze to Star. "Yes," she replied solemnly, "I will do everything I can to help your bundle find its home."

Star reached out and put her hand on Singing Wind's shoulder. "Thank you, sister."

Just then the others returned, Thunder smiling at Star. "Have you received instruction from the spirits?"

"Yes," Star said, holding up the log. "I need your help hollowing this out."

"The elk hide is tanned enough for sewing," Thunder said. "Brother's old shirt is in tatters, so we will use the hide to make him a new one. We can take turns working on the shirt and helping you."

Star smiled in agreement. "We will carve the walls down to the thickness of a thumb's width."

Whittling out the log was a tedious process since only one person at a time could fit their hand and knife in the opening. Before long, the work consisted of stabbing the core of the log and twisting out thin slivers of wood. However, by the end of the next day, they had tunneled a nearly round cavity in the cedar.

Placing the container in her lap, Star slid the symbol-covered sticks and her sacred bundle into the hollow cedar. She trimmed down the cap just enough for a tight seal. Finally, she used remaining strips of elk hide to bind the cask shut and fashioned leftover pieces as shoulder straps.

Brother appeared wearing his new elk-skin shirt and carrying a dead rabbit.

"Your trapping skills are improving, Brother," Star said approvingly. "And your shirt and black hair make you look almost Indian."

Brother smiled with pride. "I asked the animal spirits to spare a rabbit for us, as Golden Eagle told me to." He went to the stream to prepare the animal for cooking.

Star remembered back to the night when Golden Eagle's cough had alerted Brother to an intruder. *It was noble of him to charge into the darkness with only a knife to protect me and the others. Now he is asking and helping, instead of demanding and taking. His attitude toward himself, others, and Mother Earth is changing. Like Brother, the seed of humanity lies in the invaders' hearts, as it does within everyone. They, too, could awaken someday.*

Montana Territory, June 1880

Nearly a moon had passed since their days of rest in the valley, and plenty of dried elk meat allowed them to keep moving. The mountain range had turned northwest, tempting the riders to travel directly north through the open prairie. Golden Eagle knew they could double their speed on the flatlands, but he considered it too risky. His small band would lose a fight with even a handful of soldiers in the open. So, they had traveled northwest in the safety of the mountains, clambering around gulches and cliffs. Water proved plentiful in the foothills, and they found many springs and small pools along their path.

One day in the early afternoon, Golden Eagle stared northeast, barely discerning three conical shapes in the distance, and concluded they were the buttes.

He looked at the foothills, and beyond them, the vast prairie. Following Buffalo Killer's instructions had paid off. They had traveled in the mountains unnoticed for moons. Now they must continue their trek in the open.

As they rode across the prairie, Singing Wind grew more and more mystified. Flowers bloomed, and the grass stood tall and green. Where had the buffalo gone?

A gust of wind brought a fleeting smell of death. Moments later, the smell returned stronger than before. When the band crested a hill, they came upon scores of skinned buffalo. The carcasses littered the ground, lying so closely together, the horses could not pass between them. The band gave a collective gasp, then rode slowly around the grisly mass of flesh. The stench of decomposing bodies forced them to cover their noses as they rode.

Singing Wind could not believe it. In her shock, she passed by the slaughtered beasts as if imprisoned in a hideous dream. Her sadness ran so deep that no revenge or chants could counter it. She remembered warrior stories of the white men killing buffalo only for their skin, leaving the meat to rot. At other times, the whites had taken nothing, simply committing the slaughter for its own sake. The warriors had spoken truly. She knew now that the great buffalo herds would soon disappear from the prairie forever.

They rode on into the cool breeze without speaking a word. By mid-evening, the sweeping rangeland made Golden Eagle feel defenseless. If discovered, they would simply have to surrender. From this point on, he would not rest easy until they crossed the Medicine Line.

"There is a road ahead," Singing Wind called.

Golden Eagle told the others to get out of sight and rest. He dismounted, looked intently for any movement, and then ran to the road. He saw a well-traveled thoroughfare, marks of horseshoes and wagon wheels overlapping. Roads meant soldiers. Any Indian scout with the soldiers would notice the tracks of five unshod horses. His group could not easily blot out their trail as they crossed the road. He pulled up a handful of tall grass, carefully erased his tracks, and returned to the others. The band agreed to wait until sundown before moving on.

At dusk, they crossed the road. Singing Wind and Star meticulously erased their tracks a bowshot to either side. When they returned, the full moon had climbed above the horizon, casting enough light to reveal the way. Golden Eagle led the horses at a slow canter. The North Star shone clearly in the sky, assuring them every stride brought them closer to Grandmother's Land.

Midway through the night, they reached a river. Golden Eagle would rather have kept moving but chose not to risk attempting to cross the river in poor light. *Everyone will have a chance to wash up, and Thunder can comfortably nurse Young Fox.* He told everyone to shed the horses of their loads and let them graze. After bathing, they lay down, weary from the endless travel, knowing they would have only a short time to rest and regain their strength.

"How far ahead is Grandmother's Land?" Singing Wind asked.

Golden Eagle shared Buffalo Killer's directions, then added, "The buttes are still a full sun's ride away."

No one slept well during the rest of the night. At daybreak, they mounted and walked the horses into the water, then rode a few bowshots upstream to delay any trackers.

By mid-afternoon, the buttes growing in size elated the group. The westernmost butte lay farthest to the north, as Buffalo Killer had said. The length of daylight in this northern land astonished

Golden Eagle. If they kept moving at this pace, they could reach the western butte before dark, and camp safely on its slopes.

After the sun dipped below the horizon, the landscape began to lose its color in the evening shadows. The long day of traveling had exhausted both horses and riders. They had drawn close enough to the butte for Golden Eagle to see the trees and formations on its slopes. He studied the hillside thoroughly, looking for an ideal place to camp. *Anyone tracking us would have caught us by now.*

Thirsty from the heat and aware that they lacked water, he took only a swallow from his waterskin. From the short, withered grass all around, Golden Eagle concluded it had not rained for a long time. He looked ahead, where the base of the butte rounded to the northwest. Grandmother's Land, he realized, was no more than a white man's mile away! He smiled with relief. A surge of energy swelled from within as he thanked the spirits for protecting them during all their long days of travel. *Cross the Medicine Line now and make camp,* he thought, then reconsidered. *Better to camp on the butte and scout the land from above in the morning—*

"Riders!" Singing Wind cried. She pointed toward the northeastern horizon, where a faint cloud of dust was rising. Golden Eagle spotted nine horsemen, moving east.

Everyone stopped and looked toward the riders.

"Do not move!" Golden Eagle commanded. Only the breeze flapping the fringe strips against their buckskin disturbed the silence of the prairie. If they could go undetected for a few moments longer, the riders would move out of sight.

TWENTY-THREE

Montana Territory, June 1880

"Sergeant, I see dust far behind us near the Western Butte," Private Miller reported.

O'Riley raised his hand. "Company, halt!" He turned in his saddle and looked toward the pink southwestern horizon. "I don't see anything."

Miller pointed toward the southern end of the butte. "Small wisps of dust rising into the sky."

O'Riley set his good eye in that direction and looked for some time, but still saw nothing. "Anyone else see it?"

"A cloud of something was there a moment ago," Hankins said, "but it's gone now."

A small herd of buffalo might have caused it, O'Riley thought. *But it'll be a glorious day if we could kill off some savages.* He slapped his horse with the reins. "Maybe it's redskins. If it is, let's get 'em before they reach the border."

The squad turned toward the butte and followed O'Riley's lead. As they galloped west, O'Riley now clearly saw five horses with riders. They were winded and running slowly enough that his patrol would catch them before they reached the border.

"By damn," he said when he saw the group turn into a niche in the butte. *Too steep for horses.* The riders dismounted and scrambled into the foliage. *Whoever they are, they're up to no good.* O'Riley smiled. Five, against his nine. Now he had them.

When the men reached the loose horses at the foot of the butte, O'Riley recognized the black stallion at once. *My horse!* Now he knew whom he dealt with—the girls who had caused his transfer! *Tonight, they will die, and not quickly.* "Jennings, Franklin, round up the horses and watch the hillside for the redskins coming back down. Miller, Hankins, and Lutz, ride around to the north side of the butte to seal them off. Marshall, Thompson, and Malloy, follow me up the butte. Capture them alive if you can, and I'll find a proper way to send them to hell."

Midway up the hillside, Golden Eagle saw Thunder lagging behind. He heard Young Fox crying as he and Star ran back to help.

"Hush!" Thunder said sharply. Not another sound came from him.

Golden Eagle and Star each took an arm and helped Thunder up the steep slope.

The wind blew briskly as they reached a small plateau littered with stones. Brother and Singing Wind surveyed the landscape to the east and north.

"What do you see?" Golden Eagle asked sharply.

"Two riders on the prairie, rounding up our horses," Brother reported. "And four men coming toward us on foot—"

"Three riders are circling to the north," Singing Wind broke in. "If we stay here against so many guns, they will kill or capture us."

Star looked north into the twilight. "We are near Grandmother's Land. Let us run for the Medicine Line."

"Directly into the guns of our enemy?" Golden Eagle scoffed. But he quickly calmed himself. "We must decide now. For the safety of the band, I say we surrender and live. If we start firing, we will be killed."

Star shook her head. "I will fight alone before I surrender my bundle to soldiers."

"I would rather die than live at the mercy of cold-blooded enemies," Singing Wind declared.

"Brother, give me your white handkerchief," Golden Eagle said as he picked up a stick to use as a flagpole. "Use this to surrender, then tell them we held you captive. At least you can give up without fear."

"I'm not surrendering," Brother said resolutely. "I'll fight with Singing Wind and Star."

Thunder clasped Golden Eagle's arm. "I am sorry I have not told you before, but I have had a vision of us confronting the soldiers."

"You did?" Golden Eagle swung his head around in shock. "Did we survive?"

"I do not know..."

Golden Eagle wanted to hear more, but he lacked time. Four soldiers were well on their way up the hillside. "Though the spirits' message is unclear, we should follow it. Brother, take all the stones you can move and roll them down on the soldiers. That will slow their climb."

Brother picked up the smallest stones first and threw them over the bluff.

"Thunder, Singing Wind, Star—run northwest down the slope!" Golden Eagle ordered. "I will shoot as many as I can from here. You may have a chance to reach the Medicine Line; it is too dark for them to set their sights on you."

"No!" Thunder argued. "I did not see myself in the vision. And it is clear now that Star was carrying her bundle and the cradleboard." She turned to Star and said, "Give me your rifle. Take Young Fox and my bow. I will stay and fight with Golden Eagle."

"But," Star objected as she handed Thunder the rifle, "Young Fox cannot live a day without you."

"We will follow as soon as we can," Thunder assured her, giving Star her bow and seeing Brother roll a large rock toward the steep incline.

Singing Wind helped sling the cradleboard and quiver onto Star's back, next to her bundle. The two fled down the mountainside as Golden Eagle rushed to the edge of the plateau and began firing. Thunder leaned against a scraggly evergreen to steady herself, firing to divert the horsemen, but the soldiers rode toward Star and Singing Wind, flames erupting from their rifles as they shot.

Aim more slowly and carefully to improve the odds of hitting my targets. The leading horseman stopped to take steady aim. Thunder pointed her rifle at the sky just above the soldier, and found her sights. With full focus, she kept the crosshairs in line above the chamber, and slowly lowered the barrel. Compensating for wind and gravity, when her sites stopped just above his right shoulder, she fired. The man fell from his horse.

Thunder heard Brother firing his pistol, assuring her that he was still covering her and Golden Eagle.

Not slowed by the loss of their comrade, the other two riders bore down on Star at the base of the slope. Many steps behind Star, Singing Wind screamed, *"Hoka hey!"* and ran directly at the soldiers. The men swung their horses around and pointed their rifles at her. Thunder fired in a mad flurry to distract them, but in vain.

Singing Wind, only six paces from one soldier, fired her pistol and brought him down while the other horseman circled around and shot her point-blank from behind. Singing Wind dropped and rolled limply onto her back.

Apparently too far ahead to know what happened behind her, Star continued running.

Thunder fired her rifle's last bullet, and as she began to reload, saw Brother doing the same. "They're closing in on us!" he yelled.

Having reloaded, Thunder and Golden Eagle tried again to hit the last horseman. Behind them, sharp blasts of gunfire sounded no more than fifty paces away.

"Step back toward us, Brother!" Golden Eagle yelled.

Standing his ground, Brother kept shooting. Amid the gunfire, he shouted, "I got one!"

Thunder turned to Golden Eagle. "We cannot hit anything in such little light."

Brother ran past her. "I'll shoot the soldier!"

"Get back here, Brother!" she yelled. But he kept running down the slope, faster than she had ever seen him run before. "We must catch Brother before he reaches the horseman."

"The foot soldiers are near," Golden Eagle countered. "I hope my last bullet will kill one before we retreat. Provide Brother cover from here."

Thunder fired at the horseman, but the bullets went to waste in such poor light. She saw the mounted soldier halt before Brother, forcing him to turn back. Thunder kept firing, but the soldier held his ground. Cocking her rifle again, she saw Brother plant his feet, raise the pistol with both hands, and fire twice. Both shots missed. A flame erupted from the soldier's rifle, and Brother twisted sideways and tumbled to the ground.

A bullet whizzed through the air from behind. Looking back, Thunder saw three soldiers emerging from the brush. She whirled around behind the evergreen as Golden Eagle shot the frontrunner in the stomach. The man balled up and fell, screaming.

Flinging his empty rifle at the two approaching Bluecoats, Golden Eagle rushed to Thunder's side. "Run for the Medicine Line!" He and Thunder sprinted down the slope amid a flurry of bullets and quickly outran the winded soldiers.

Star raced across the flat ground, Singing Wind's war cry ringing in her mind. She heard gunfire but soon realized no one was chasing her. *Where is Singing Wind?* She turned back toward the battle. Through the deepening gloom, she saw the silhouette of a mounted soldier, aiming his rifle at the ground. Thinking the horseman was about to shoot one of her helpless friends, she raised her bow. Despite the rider's distance, she aimed at the figure and prayed as she let an arrow fly. She missed, and the alerted soldier turned his horse and began to shoot in her direction. She dropped to the ground to protect Young Fox and herself from bullets and sent more arrows at the soldier.

Running at full speed in the waning light, Thunder saw a prone body ahead. A few strides later, she recognized Singing Wind, staring upward with lifeless eyes. *She laid down her life for us. We can only repay her by fighting for our freedom.* Ahead of Thunder, the horseman fired in the opposite direction, his back to her. Since she had fired seven of the eight bullets she'd loaded, her next shot had to kill.

Golden Eagle caught up to her. "Cover me." He sprinted noiselessly to the mounted soldier. Springing up, he kicked the soldier's left stirrup from under his foot and pulled him from his horse. The soldier fired a shot into the air as Golden Eagle lunged for his rifle.

Hearing rapid footsteps of two men behind her, Thunder turned and fired at the closest soldier, bringing him down. The other man fired his pistol, and the bullet zinged past her head. She threw her empty rifle at him and charged for his weapon. Instantly recognizing the soldier's stench, she shouted, "Polecat!" and attacked him like a bee-stung grizzly. *Finally, my chance to kill him!*

She grabbed his pistol with both hands and pushed it down while spinning her body between his torso and his hand. She had pried two of Polecat's fingers from his gun when he clawed the back of her scalp, seized her hair, and yanked her head to the ground.

"I'm sending you to hell, you little horse-stealing bitch!" he yelled, dropping to one knee and pushing her face into the dirt. He wrenched the gun until the barrel pointed at the side of her face, but when he squeezed the trigger, it clicked uselessly.

Thunder, head pinned to the ground, twisted her body on its side. "You will die at my hand for killing my family and friends!" She pelted him with her fists and kneed him repeatedly in the abdomen and groin.

Polecat slammed down onto her, pinning her with his enormous weight. Thunder tried but failed to wiggle from under him as he sat astride her. In a fit of rage, he drew back his arm holding the pistol, and Thunder raised her arms to her head. He smacked his pistol into her forearms and across her face. "You're the whore," he bellowed, striking her again, "who clawed my eye!"

He grabbed her left arm and held it down, while continuing to swing his pistol into her face. "You ruined my life!" he roared, then lowered his voice to a hideous, breathy murmur. "You're the one who's gonna die."

Thunder squirmed, coughing and spitting dirt, trying to slide from under Polecat, but his tremendous bulk outmatched her strength. One solid blow of his gun would knock her unconscious. Then he could easily kill her, and therefore Young Fox. *I must kill him now!*

Thunder turned her head and body away from the next blow. She brought her right arm to her side to pull out her knife, but Polecat's knee blocked her reach. A direct blow to the back of her head brought a blaze of pain. As his arm swung off to one side, Thunder called on her warrior spirit's help as she threw all her strength into twisting her hips in a sideways jolt. Dislodged from his knees, Polecat tumbled and lost hold of her arm. She whipped out her knife and sliced his chest as he rolled away.

Polecat stood and looked at the blood oozing onto his slashed clothes. He dropped his empty pistol and pulled out his knife.

Thunder sprang up and circled in the direction of Polecat's bad eye. *One mistake, and he is dead. But he might wound me before dying.*

Suddenly, Golden Eagle charged Polecat from the side and knocked him several paces away. Thunder ran over as Golden Eagle grabbed Polecat's knife hand and they rolled on the ground. When Golden Eagle shifted out of the way, Thunder crouched down and rammed her knife into Polecat's chest. She launched into a flurry of stabs—for how long, she did not know.

Her knife-wielding arm ached from exhaustion, but she didn't stop until her body refused to go on. Finally, she sat back on her haunches to see Golden Eagle standing over her.

"He is the bastard who killed our people!" Thunder whispered fiercely. Polecat's scarred eye stared lifelessly into the evening gloom.

Golden Eagle kicked Polecat's head. It flopped sideways, facing away from them. "Now my father's soul is set free."

Thunder stood. "And Grandfather's, Young Falcon's, Little Bird's, and so many others."

"Leave Polecat for the coyotes," Golden Eagle said. "We must find Young Fox and Star."

They started to run for the border, but before they reached a full sprint, Thunder saw a crumpled body in a blood-covered shirt. "Brother!" They fell on hands and knees before him.

Fresh blood oozed from his chest. He was unconscious but still breathing.

"We must take him north," Thunder implored in a high-pitched whisper. "The two other soldiers may come to the battlefield!"

Golden Eagle nodded, grabbed Brother's shoulders, and lifted the limp body. He draped one arm over his shoulders, and Thunder ducked under the other arm. Hearing Young Fox crying in the distance, Thunder knew exactly where to go.

After they had lugged Brother a couple of bowshots beyond the battlefield, Golden Eagle said between pants, "I think we are safe. Should we not tend to Brother now?"

"Moving Brother after treating him will reopen his wound. We must get him to Star as quickly as we can."

TWENTY-FOUR

Northwest Territories, Canada, June 1880

"His back is bleeding terribly," Star said over Young Fox's crying. "We need something to hold back the flow."

Golden Eagle pulled off his shirt and held it firmly over Brother's wound. Thunder pulled Golden Eagle's knife from its sheath and quickly cut off both her and Star's sleeves.

"He will breathe more easily if we turn him over," Star said. As they carefully rolled Brother onto his back, she felt wetness on his chest. "The bullet passed through him," she said grimly as she pressed the sleeves against the wound. "I have medicine, but do we have a flint and water to prepare it?"

"What is left in our canteens," Thunder said as she took Young Fox from the cradleboard and began nursing him. "We left everything else on the horses." She handed the knife back to Golden Eagle.

Star gave a long, heavy sigh. "I have little hope he will survive without the proper treatments."

Working in nearly complete darkness, they could only hope to hold back the bleeding. They chanted for the spirits to keep Brother alive. Finally, far into the night, the bleeding stopped. Under the waning moon, the three lay around the boy, each with a hand on him, lending him their precious remaining strength. They waited out the night, praying for Brother and telling Star the details of the battle as she tended him in the moonlight. Upon learning of Singing Wind's death, Star forced herself to delay her grief to focus on the living boy who needed her.

As the darkness gave way to dawn, two soldiers rode around the butte from the east. The riders led five horses carrying the band's belongings, and four Army horses with gear. Star quickly alerted the others.

Thunder sprang up, cupped her hands, and yelled, "Sto-o-ormy-y!"

The proud animal whinnied and reared on his hind legs, breaking the soldier's grip on his rope. Still bridled and saddled, he danced a complete circle, then raced directly for Thunder.

When he reached her waiting arms, his nostrils fluttered in obvious delight. He nestled his head against her, and his gentle neighing reminded her of a camp puppy whining for attention. She rubbed the favorite place between his ears and patted his nose. Looking him in the eye, she said, "We need you as much as ever. We are so happy you are back with us."

Thunder's cry had woken Young Fox, so Star picked him up and joined Thunder, Stormy, and Golden Eagle. Star turned her eyes to the Bluecoats. "Shall we try to get our horses and belongings?"

Golden Eagle shook his head. "The two soldiers have a pistol and rifle each, and plenty of bullets. All we have are knives and a few arrows. We would die before we got close."

"Why do they not come for us, then?"

"We are a few hundred paces north of the butte, so we must be in Grandmother's Land. Besides, they do not know how many weapons we have, and we outnumber them."

The soldiers arrived near the six corpses then looked up the mountain. They led the eight horses uphill and returned a short time later, two of the horses carrying a body each. The men loaded the weapons and dead onto the other horses then looked at Singing Wind's corpse. They spoke to each other for a moment, and finally stooped over and loaded the body. They rode away, leaving the hillside bare.

Thunder looked to Golden Eagle. "Why did they take her?"

"We will never know," Golden Eagle rasped.

"Surely the Great Spirit will provide a good place for her in the Other World," Star said despondently.

"Did you hear her war cry when you passed the soldiers?"

"Yes. But I had to protect Young Fox, so I did not dare break my stride to look back."

Golden Eagle nodded. "It looked to me as if Singing Wind sacrificed herself to save your lives."

"Why do you think so?"

"The soldiers were aiming at you when Singing Wind gave her war cry and charged them. She diverted their attention from you to herself."

Star sat silently, looking down. "If I had not needed to protect Young Fox, I would have stayed and fought with her."

"She killed a soldier before the other shot her in the back," Golden Eagle said gently. "By then you had run far away."

"When I returned to camp after my vision, I asked Singing Wind to help me protect my bundle. But I never thought she would have to give her life for my mission."

"I am grateful to her for keeping Young Fox safe," Thunder said with a heavy heart.

Brother struggled for every breath, but he breathed, none-theless. Star took a piece of buckskin from her herb pouch. Despite their great thirst, Star drained the near-empty waterskins, soaking the hide to relieve Brother's fever.

Lacking Singing Wind's body for a funeral ceremony, they could only recite chants to pass her spirit to the Other World. The chants would likely not help her much, but nothing else could be done. Afterward, they shared pleasant memories of their friend.

The faint gurgling of Brother's breathing was the only sound on the prairie. Only clumps of grass and a few half-buried stones lay here and there across the nearly treeless land.

Star returned to caring for Brother. "I need water to keep his fever down."

Golden Eagle nodded in agreement, then got to his feet and took the waterskins. After mounting Stormy, he turned the stallion north and rode off.

Thunder felt the heat from the sun and knew its strong rays would soon worsen Brother's condition. If she collected rocks and piled them on each side of him to set the cradleboard on, it would provide some shade. She left Young Fox in the cradleboard next to Brother and stayed within hearing range. While picking up stones, she wondered if she could use one as a flint, but none were suit-able. Upon finishing the rock piles, she took Young Fox from the cradleboard, placed it over Brother, and went to collect grass to weave for a more permanent shade.

Star loosened Brother's shirt to look more closely at his wound. While drawing the elk-skin open, she felt a lump in his pocket, and took it out. "Thunder, I found Brother's flint!

"That's wonderful!" Thunder cried. "Now all we need is water to make the medicine."

Star checked for her knife, but the sheath was empty. The knife must have fallen out the previous night. Brother's knife had also disappeared. She called again to Thunder, "Where is your teacher's bone-handled skinning knife?"

"I left it in Polecat's chest."

"Oh, then we will have to use Golden Eagle's knife to spark a fire when he returns."

Moments later, Golden Eagle rode in, dismounted, and lifted bulging waterskins from Stormy's back. Thunder looked, wide-eyed. "You found water already? I did not expect you to be back so soon."

"A river lies to the north. After riding a short time, I saw a line of trees in the distance and rode until I reached its banks."

"Give me your knife," Star said. "I need to start a fire."

Later, after treating Brother with mugwort and comfrey, Star knew Brother needed further help from herbs. Her friend, the plant of a thousand leaves—if freshly gathered—would be her best aid to heal Brother. But it might be difficult to find.

Without thinking, she swung the cedar log on her back, and mounted Stormy. "I need to find the plant of a thousand leaves today, or Brother may die."

"I will have more firewood ready to heat the medicine when you return," Golden Eagle assured her.

"I will tend to Brother while you are gone," Thunder called as Star rode off.

After a short ride, Star reached the river. She slowly walked Stormy upstream, hoping to find a large patch of the plant to help Brother in the days to come.

The sun arced above her as she crossed the river many times looking for her plant friend on both banks. Far from camp, she saw the sun had journeyed halfway down to the horizon. *I had better look on foot, settle for one plant, and come back another day.* She dismounted and left Stormy to graze.

While going along a bend of the river, she studied the foliage for several hundred paces when she came upon a patch of thousand-leaved plants. "Thank you," she whispered as she knelt and pulled several out of the ground. After carefully removing the dirt from the roots, she used prairie grass to wrap the plants into a tight bunch. As she stood, she looked up and caught sight of a magnificent cliff towering high over the river. *The wall of stone from my vision!*

Star ran, retracing the steps she had taken following the deer. Everything matched with uncanny perfection. Behind the wall, a vast array of rock projections covered the ground. Some stone masses resembled towers, and others rose more gently like small hills. All displayed layering in shape and subtle patterns, as if revealing different ages in the life of Mother Earth.

Star hurried to the mound of stone that would hold her sacred bundle. Now she knew why she had brought the cedar log without thinking: the spirits had guided her. Her life's journey raced through her mind, and she realized every decision had brought her to this place, this moment.

When she took the cedar log from her back, she felt a tremendous burden lifting from her. She looked at the clear sky and saw birds flying in the vast expanse. As far as she could see, green covered the land, dotted by flowers in full bloom. She had brought the sacred bundle to its home.

Here, among the teeming life, she and her friends could find all that they desired. Along the river lay plenty of plants, wildlife, and stone to make shelter and weapons. They needed nothing more than what Maheo had always provided.

Fulfilling her life's duty, Star reverently slid the bundle deep into the round cavity.

The bundle will wait here, patiently, her spirit whispered, *until people are ready to reclaim their souls.*

TWENTY-FIVE

Northwest Territories, Canada, June 1880

The band used branches and prairie grass to build a shelter around Brother. They also made a sled, and when Brother had recovered enough, they brought him north to the riverbank.

Star gathered a new medicine bundle to assist her in healing Brother, and over the course of a moon, his health continued to improve. As soon as he could take short walks around camp, the group began their journey east in search of Sitting Bull's encampment. Still in pain, Brother rode in the sled pulled by Stormy. The others walked.

One evening after a half-moon of travel, they stopped for the night on a riverbank. Star and Thunder, with Young Fox on her back, set out to find firewood, and Golden Eagle unharnessed Stormy. Brother collapsed on the bank, staring glumly into the water, reproaching himself. *I didn't listen to Thunder and got shot.*

Because of me, we are moving at half the speed of when we traveled north. They all hate me. He looked to Golden Eagle. "I'm sorry to burden all of you."

"Don't think that way," Golden Eagle said cheerfully. "We are all very happy to see you healing so quickly."

"But what will happen when we meet Sitting Bull's people? Will you abandon me?"

"You will never be alone," Golden Eagle assured him. "You showed your heart to us in battle. Whatever the future brings, you are welcome at my side."

"I should have returned to you when Thunder yelled to me," Brother lamented. "But I was sure I'd kill one soldier with two bullets and clear our way to Canada."

"Strange things happen in battle," Golden Eagle said with a smile. "That is why warriors need years of training."

"I wish I could learn more warrior skills now, but I can't."

Golden Eagle laughed. "You have a lifetime to learn."

Despite his misgivings, Brother began to laugh too, but the pain in his chest made him stop. He smiled, relieved he had a future with friends.

During the next half-moon, the band followed an east-flowing river and found just enough food to stave off their hunger. Brother could now ride on Stormy's back for parts of the day. They traveled through a woodland where game should have abounded, but hunting proved fruitless. Their traps and snares caught little. When Golden Eagle began to see footprints and horse tracks, he concluded the land had been overhunted. *Maybe Sitting Bull's settlement is near.*

Three suns later, toward dusk, he saw a column of smoke rising and thought it was probably from a cooking fire. He spied another plume of smoke farther east, and a moment later, he saw another much farther to the north. "It is an enormous camp," he said excitedly to the others while pointing to the smoke plumes, "if these fires are all from the same village."

Finally, they came upon a great encampment of weather-beaten tipis. So many lodges dotted the woods, Golden Eagle could not see where they ended. A cluster of twenty tipis bulged out from the outskirts of the settlement. The rich aroma of cooking stew made the famished travelers' mouths water.

A woman of thirty winters, with Sioux markings on her clothes, glanced at the band. Star walked over to her cautiously. "I am Falling Star, Cheyenne," she said respectfully, in Sioux. "My friends and I have fled the land of the Bluecoats, and we seek refuge among you."

"The people of Sitting Bull's encampment welcome you," the woman said cheerfully. "My name is Running Elk. Unsaddle your horse and eat with us."

The white boy in Indian clothes climbing down from the huge stallion seemed to intrigue three children near Running Elk who looked at them and smiled. They peppered Brother with questions, and he answered impressively in his smattering of Sioux and Cheyenne.

"My children," Running Elk explained. "My husband left with a group of warriors today on a buffalo hunt south of the Medicine Line."

"Back to the land of the Bluecoats?" Star asked. "Is that not very dangerous?"

"Yes. If soldiers catch them, they could be shot." Running Elk pointed to her ragged tipi. "But we could surely use the meat and hides for winter."

Later, she served the newcomers in her tipi. They ate the stew ravenously and stopped only when their stomachs neared bursting.

After thanking Running Elk for the meal, Star put down her bowl and said, "White Blade and his band should be here. Do you know anything about them?"

When Running Elk said nothing, Star asked, "Is it bad news?"

"We have heard White Blade and his people were on their way north when Colonel Edwards' army attacked them. The soldiers killed many, captured the others, and took them to a reservation."

Star bowed her head. "Now even fewer Cheyenne live to carry on my culture. Perhaps I could have helped them."

"The soldiers are so many now," Thunder consoled, "and their weapons are more powerful than ever."

Star nodded.

Golden Eagle wondered if Crossing Wolf and Two Feathers had survived. If so, they would be confined to a reservation. He remembered their faces as he departed from them at White Blade's lodge, and grief settled in his heart. He held little hope of ever seeing them again.

Later, Running Elk told Star that her tipi could hold everyone, including her family. She invited the exhausted travelers to stay. The offer thrilled them, and they accepted with gratitude.

In the middle of the night, a multitude of gunshots brought everyone in the tipi to their feet. They rushed out to see armed Sioux warriors running to mount horses while yelling war cries.

"What is happening?" Star asked.

Running Elk reentered the tipi. When the others joined her, she said, "My family came here with Sitting Bull's people three years ago. Our village seems set apart because many chiefs and their people have left for food on the reservations. From the beginning of the settlement, mostly Lakota have lived here. An Oglala Sioux band of Crazy Horse's followers arrived soon after soldiers killed him in custody. Men of many tribes travel here and bring their women, children, and wounded. We welcome everyone and share our food and shelter. But few have come in the last year.

"Though all we want to do is live here in peace, the U.S. Army works against us in every possible way. They try to turn the Canadian leaders against us and our chiefs against one another, with some success. All summer long, they have been burning prairie grass south of the Medicine Line so no buffalo would cross. Local tribes such as the Cree, and Assiniboine attack our village, trying to steal our small reserve of food. That was the commotion, but these skirmishes seldom cause harm. Still, without more buffalo, we have little food and clothing for the cold season. We may have no choice but to cross the Medicine Line, surrender to the U.S. Army, and be put on a reservation."

The newcomers groaned at the plight of the refugees.

Thunder could only imagine Running Elk's sadness—her people trading freedom for sustenance, like her grandfather once did.

One warm day, Star came to Thunder carrying a basket, ready to gather roots and greens.

After Thunder put Young Fox in his cradleboard and onto her back, they went to a nearby meadow. Crouching amid the tall greenery, they filled the basket. Thunder smiled, remembering their good times together.

"As you know," Star said, "I often go about the encampment, healing the sick. When I tell them about you and Golden Eagle, it makes them sad neither of you has a family. But when I tell them your story, it warms their hearts."

Somewhat surprised, Thunder said, "I am pleased the tale has given them something, however small, in return for their hospitality."

"But they want to give you something more," Star said in a lively tone, "and so does Running Elk. They want to welcome us all here by holding a Sioux wedding ceremony for you and Golden Eagle."

Thunder remained quiet for a moment. She had never wished for an elaborate ceremony, seen by so many. Other than an agreement between the couple's family and an exchange of gifts, Apache weddings practically did not exist. *But now Golden Eagle and I live with a different people. We all need to establish new ways, and Star leading a new wedding ceremony would begin the transformation.*

Star continued. "In about twenty sleeps, when summer ends, they will hold a celebration on the day of equal light and darkness. Some people say that as a good time to celebrate the harvest here in the north. It is a very important time."

"I think," Thunder said slowly, "you have a very good idea. 'The day of equal light and darkness,'" she repeated.

Star nodded, her smile widening. "That is perfect. The two of you will join together at the time of harvest and reap what you have sown."

Thunder beamed. *Star said it more beautifully than even I could. How wonderful it is to have such a close friend.* After a moment, she asked, "Will you conduct the ceremony?"

"I will with pleasure." Star turned to face Thunder. "For all my days, I will treasure the honor of uniting you and Golden Eagle."

They returned to working in silence, and Thunder weighed the idea of sharing her secret. Finally, she said, "I think I am carrying Golden Eagle's child. It is too early to be sure, but I believe it."

Star turned back to Thunder, a look of astonishment on her face. "You are?" she said, amazed.

Giddy with simple joy, Thunder began to laugh.

Star shared her laughter. When it subsided, she continued. "This will be another great soul, like Young Fox."

Thunder nodded. *Raising a family with Golden Eagle would make my grandfather very happy. To grow up with a sibling may make him more so.*

"So how will you provide for two growing children?" Star asked. "Would you consider going south with most of the others to live on a reservation?"

"Why?" Thunder snorted in disgust. "We might live in uncertainty here in the north, but so will those who go. The soldiers might give them enough to eat, or they might not. At least here we can live as free people, trusting in the spirits. There we would have to trust in agency masters and teachers who know nothing but think they know everything. No, Golden Eagle and I will stay, even though we might have to fight again in the future. The whites in this land could turn against us, and so could the other tribes. We do not know what we will face, but free people never do. Singing Wind sacrificed herself for our freedom, and I will live free in her honor."

"And so you should," Star said. "But you and your children will risk much danger if you raise them alone."

Thunder shook her head. "Not alone. Brother will certainly stay with us. Also, others here in the village might stay or leave with us if they choose."

"It is best to stay free. I wish you well."

Young Fox began to cry, and Star rushed over and took him from the cradleboard.

"What do you mean?" Thunder asked. "Will you leave us? Star, you are part of our family too. You are my sister, and I hate the thought of raising my children without your wisdom."

"I will be with you from time to time," Star said as she held Young Fox, now quiet. "I will always be there when you need me, I promise you."

Numb, Thunder asked the first question that came to mind. "But where will you go?"

"Powers and vision grow within me even now. In the past, I could help only those whom I found by chance. Now my intuition is strong enough to go directly to those in need. I will walk the northern land and heal the ones who suffer."

Thunder looked at her, confused.

Star grinned. "But not before the wedding," she said cheerfully, "and, of course, I will be there to deliver your next baby!"

Preparation for Golden Eagle and Thunder's wedding raced at a feverish pitch. Star found a wet nurse to care for Young Fox on that day, and she also volunteered to make garments for Thunder and Golden Eagle as her gift to them. The Sioux took the other festival preparations upon themselves. One group constructed a new lodge for the soon-to-be newlyweds. Another group built a temporary lodge, outside the camp, for the couple's use after the wedding. Running Elk organized the food preparation. Brother accepted the task of grooming and adorning Stormy for the day of the ceremony.

Star purified the ground at the center of the village for the ritual. She also told Thunder and Golden Eagle about the particulars of the ceremony she had planned. She would marry them in mostly Sioux fashion, but with enough differences to make their joining a unique one.

The village spent the wedding day in celebration. Ignoring the meagerness of their food supplies, they feasted on their best. Children played games, and the finely-dressed adults gathered to share stories and gamble. Late that afternoon, the women and girls danced.

Just before sunset, Golden Eagle went to the open area at the center of the village. He stopped in front of an array of logs resting against one another, like the poles of a tipi, and flanked by two unlit torches.

A moment later, Thunder came to his side. She looked resplendent in her deerskin dress, and a pleasant tinkling came from the tiny bells on the fringe of her sleeves. Garlands of beads laced with flowers hung from her shoulders and across her chest. Many necklaces hung around her neck, including a medallion similar to the one she had made for Golden Eagle. Silver bracelets embedded with onyx and turquoise stones encircled her wrists. Golden Eagle smiled when he noticed the tops of her moccasins, beaded in the shape of thunderbirds.

The sight of Thunder brought back memories of the first time he had seen her. She had grown, but her deep brown eyes and gleaming black hair held as much allure as ever.

Star came and stood between the torches. She wore a fringed buckskin dress and a garland of flowers around her neck.

Thunder turned her gaze from Star to Golden Eagle. His totem, a flying eagle, painted in gold, adorned the front of his buffalo-skin shirt. Over the hide, he wore Thunder's medallion around his neck.

Star lit the torches and proclaimed, "The marriage ceremony has begun."

Four Sioux warriors approached and stood next to the couple. They raised a large blanket over their heads, each man holding a corner. Golden Eagle and Thunder stepped under the blanket, and Star took a bundle of silver sage and held it in the flame of one of the torches. When the sage began to smoke, Star circled the blanket, waving the bundle. Thunder put her arm around Golden Eagle's waist and squeezed as she breathed in the enlivening aroma. Star led them around the village, and many people congratulated them and followed.

Suddenly Brother appeared, stepping through the crowd, carrying Young Fox.

Taking her baby, she saw his expression of joy, and hugged him close to her body. She carried Young Fox while resuming her walk at the head of the procession, which now included hundreds of followers.

It was almost dark when Thunder and Golden Eagle returned to the two burning torches. Thunder gave Young Fox back to Brother, and the couple simultaneously picked up the torches and put them into the dry wood. Fire sprang up, growing quickly until it lit up the area.

They bowed as Star brought the burning sage bundle over her cupped hand in which she held fresh wildflower petals. She blew the smoke and petals upward. They swirled and fluttered back down, onto and around the couple. "Your hearts now beat as one, your breaths flow as one, your voices speak as one."

Thunder and Golden Eagle straightened, clasped hands, and slipped through the crowd. He effortlessly lifted her onto Stormy's back then mounted behind her. Thunder breathed in deeply, and joy spread throughout her being. She thought of her mother and rubbed her perfect-fitting turquoise bracelet. *I wish she could have seen the ceremony. She would have been so pleased.* Thunder ran her fingers along the bracelet until she touched the newly added arrowhead, recovered by the man who had never stopped searching for her.

Star saw Thunder smile when Golden Eagle whispered something in her ear. After they rode off in the fading twilight, she looked around at the dispersing crowd. The affirmation of life during the wedding ceremony had buoyed them up, briefly liberating them from their troubles and pains.

As the mood of communal joining faded, the people retreated to their homes. Now, more than ever, Star saw all that they had suffered. Grief had etched into their faces like the symbols burned into the hickory sticks in her bundle. One man ached from the loss of his wife, who had been murdered by soldiers. Another had escaped from a reservation, but only after illness had claimed his family. Still, others pined for those who had died or those whom the soldiers had captured. Many would return to reservations just to provide food and shelter for their young children or old parents. Star knew only a very few, like herself, had escaped the whites to live out their lives free.

She walked out of the village, deep into the woods. Closing her eyes, she envisioned those who lived near and far. People beyond count, in the next village or in lands beyond her knowledge, needed her help. She would travel to them and serve the Great Spirit by aiding them.

Her old friend, the magnificent deer, appeared before her and looked into her eyes. He turned, trotted a short distance—then vanished. This time, Star understood what the deer had done. She took one step after him and suddenly found herself in another place. She stood on sacred ground atop the Devil's Tower, under a black sky ablaze with stars.

Her spirit liberated by this holy ground, Star's vision grew more far-reaching. She could now look upon any place on the sunlit earth at any moment, any age. Time passed quickly, and she watched generations of Cheyenne living on reservations. The whites had torn them from their heritage, leaving them adrift from the knowledge of their forebears. Tears welled in her eyes as she saw the prophecy of Sweet Medicine come to pass. Nearly all the people would live in poverty, struggling to preserve their cultures. Never would they know the native plants, animals, and vast lands from which their traditions had sprung forth and thrived. They would lead a life even more difficult than their ancestors, during her time on earth.

Time slowed. Something pulled Star's gaze downward, to a single place. Her spirit hovered over a poor Cheyenne community far in the future. The sun shone in a clear sky as children played on the parched earth. In a wooded hill on the outskirts of the village, a deer stood watching over them.

Star felt the beckoning of her totem, and opened herself to his message:

Under their brown skin will still beat a warm heart pumping the blood of the ancients. It will take generations for them to realize the teachings of their grandfathers are still true. Only then, the purpose for which they lived and died will begin to be understood.

And a new breed will evolve.

DISCUSSION QUESTIONS

Talks Like Thunder

1) What was your first impression of Gray Fox and how did your opinion of him change as you read? How much do you think 21st-century expectations impacted your opinion of Gray Fox as a character?

2) What similarities exist between the lifestyle of an "average" American child and Talks Like Thunder?

3) How might Talks Like Thunder's journey through this novel have been different if she had not been trained as a warrior?

Falling Star

4) Which is more important to Talk Like Thunder and to Falling Star, traditions or people?

5) Which relationship in this novel was the most transformative for Talks Like Thunder?

6) How does the guilt and shame Talks Like Thunder experiences, after her rape in *Falling Star*, compare to the feelings contemporary rape victims feel? How much of her reaction do you think was influenced by her culture and how much was influenced by human psychology?

Singing Wind

7) In chapter five, the author humanizes the white soldiers. Does this treatment of the soldier characters make you more empathetic towards the white people in the novel? Why or why not?

8) The treatment of buffalo is mentioned multiple times through the end of the text. How does this treatment mimic the way white people treated Native Americans?

9) Look at the character of Brother in *Singing Wind*. How is Brother's journey influenced by the idea of hope?

10) When should cultural and religious traditions die and/or be adapted?

Marjorie Carter was born in Salem, Missouri, on July 17, 1937. Of Cherokee descent, she learned the traditional ways of her relatives from early childhood. During the eight grade, she was forced to leave school to work and provide for her younger brothers. At the age of nineteen, she moved to Texas and began her careers in the restaurant and real estate businesses. During her life, she was diagnosed with seven different cancers and fought against melanoma for 25 years. A Native American seer and shaman, she had a passion for art, poetry, and stories. She wrote at her ranch near San Miguel de Allende, Mexico, hoping that Red With Native Blood would help reservation students embrace their heritage. Marjorie died of pneumonia on July 12, 2004.

Randal Nerhus received a BS in Agricultural Studies from Iowa State University in 1982, and an MA in Oriental Philosophy and Religion from Bananas Hindu University, India, in 1988. Shortly after obtaining his agricultural degree, he volunteered with the Peace Corps in the Philippines. While traveling in the mountains on the island of Palawan, he visited a remote tribal village and encountered a very different way of life—one of community, contentment, happiness, and love. Fifteen years later, his interest in tribal traditions deepened while taking part in a ManKind Project initiation that used native approaches to bring men into a life of integrity. In 2002, Marjorie Carter took him under her shamanic guidance which complemented and expanded on his early Christian foundations. From 2013 to 2016, he lived in Colombia's Amazon jungle studying under Cocama shaman don Rogelio Carihuasari, and relevant parts of that experience were incorporated into the trilogy.

FURTHER INFORMATION

Learn more about the *Red With Native Blood* series, as well as news and events at:

Randalnerhus.com

Facebook: Randal Nerhus-Red With Native Blood

@RandalNerhus on Twitter

RandalNerhus on Instagram

Randal Nerhus on LinkedIn

Randal Nerhus on TikTok

Printed in Great Britain
by Amazon